# White Chin

## The Cat that Walked by his Wild Lone

# White Chin

## The Cat that Walked by his Wild Lone

# Marilyn Edwards

*with illustrations by* **France Bauduin**

Catnip

CATNIP BOOKS
Published by Catnip Publishing Ltd
14 Greville Street
London
EC1N 8SB

This edition first published 2010

1 3 5 7 9 10 8 6 4 2

Text copyright © Marilyn Edwards 2010
Illustrations copyright © France Bauduin 2010
The moral rights of the author and illustrator have been asserted.

A CIP catalogue record for this book is available from the British Library.

ISBN 978-1-84647-105-6

Printed in Poland

www.catnippublishing.co.uk

To my father, with love

"When the moon gets up and night comes . . .
he goes out to the Wet Wild Woods . . .
waving his wild tail and walking by his wild lone."

From 'The Cat that Walked by Himself' by Rudyard Kipling

collected in *Just So Stories* (1902)

# CONTENTS

# 1

## Out into the wet wild woods

An old grey car drove up the hill towards the gate that led into High Fell Wood. The road ended here and the car paused. Slowly it edged forward in a circle, its wheels crunching over leaves and fir cones, until it faced downhill again. It stopped. The engine fell silent. After a few moments the driver's door opened and two large feet clad in trainers emerged. A tall man wearing jeans and a football shirt climbed out, stretched himself and turned to look up at the trees towering above him.

The wind was blowing in warm gusts from the west and the air was heavy with moisture, carrying a rich smell of damp earth and rotting leaves. Thin sunlight filtered through the tree tops, picking out the russet and gold of the autumn leaves.

A wood mouse rustled through the undergrowth of the forest floor. Every so often she would squat back on her hind legs, twitching her nose while she stared around her. Absent-mindedly she tweaked her ears and whiskers with her forepaws. She was nervous. The little wood mouse was pregnant with her last litter of the year and had done well to escape the attentions of the many creatures who stalked these woods, all of whom might at any time consider her a delicious meal. She was busy gathering food into small piles to take back to her burrow under the roots of an oak tree. At this time of year the trees were teeming with nuts and as a small creature she had learned to watch out that she didn't get hit on the head by them as treeborne creatures made them bounce to earth. Squirrels were the worst; in their haste they dropped as many nuts as they collected.

As the wood mouse squeezed through the tangle of tree roots, struggling with the awkward bulk of a prized acorn, she missed the distant voices of the two men talking as they stood by their car. Their presence, however, did not go unnoticed by two watchful rooks and one called out a warning 'kaw, kaw, kaw' to his distant companion, who replied in kind. The taller of the men, the one who had been driving, pulled out a sack from the back seat and tossed it, carelessly, over his shoulder. They hurried off up the steep path into the wood and as they walked, the sack on the man's shoulder wriggled around in a squirmy sort of way. Whatever was in it was squeaking a great deal.

The young man panted noisily as he half-ran up the hill behind his big-striding companion. Neither of them noticed the young girl looking down at them, hidden amidst a dark group of trees. Kirstie had been watching them since their car first started crawling up the hill. As their voices came nearer, she wiggled herself into the middle of a thick bush, fingering loose strands of long auburn hair back into a knot so it didn't fly out and give her away. She was curious. What on earth was in that sack? She listened hard. Their voices weren't local. The younger man had put out his hand and was tugging at the shirt of the other, trying to get his attention.

'Hey, listen – do you think he'll survive out here, or even last the night? He's not very old is he?'

'Old enough!' The bigger man swung round sharply and pointed a finger at his questioner. 'Look here, let's just get this straight, shall we? I wanted to drown him, remember. It was *your* blinking idea to let him out in some wild wood somewhere, so this one is strictly down to you, mate.'

The younger man pulled his shoulders up around his neck and stuck out his lower lip. He looked up at the dark swaying trees and wrinkled his forehead.

'This place gives me the creeps big time. I wouldn't fancy being left here,' he said in a whiny voice.

'Well, you're not being left here,' the older man

called over his shoulder, the sack bumping against him as he moved ahead. He looked back and raised his eyebrows as he registered the look of doubt on the lad's face. He turned to face him and shouted crossly, 'But if you carry on like this that's exactly what I'll do. I *will* bloomin' well leave you here! *You* wanted to come. And besides, these woods are nice, *very* nice – as you may discover one day if you play your cards right. So nice we might even make a special trip back sometime soon and get to know the place really well.'

'Oh, that sort of trip. Really? Are these the woods where you do it then?'

'They might be, but you just keep your lip buttoned. You never know who might be listening.'

Kirstie pulled back further into her bush, shivering. She wondered just how long she might have to stay there. She was getting cramp. The older man dropped the sack roughly on the ground and bent down out of the wind to light a cigarette.

'Trees have ears you know.' He laughed unpleasantly and stood up. He threw the sack roughly over his back again and walked on a few hundred yards before he stopped and turned the sack upside down, tipping its wriggling contents on the ground.

Kirstie stood on tiptoes, risking all, to peer through the protective branches of her bush. What emerged from the sack was a protesting tangle of black-and-white legs and a tail. As she watched she saw one young, unhappy cat stand up, miaow and then shake himself.

Each of his long legs ended in a white sock. He had a white chest, neck and tummy, and a distinctive white, off-centre patch on his chin. The man holding the sack kicked out hard at the little cat with his foot.

'Shove off White Chin, and good riddance. What the wife and kids don't know, won't hurt 'em. I'll be happy never to see you again.'

White Chin fell forward as the man's foot lifted his rear end and he mewled out in pain. He blinked his eyes in the sudden light – and – realising he was free, his mournful whimper changed into a gleeful miaow and he scampered off a few feet in triumph. The men glanced at his back briefly, nodded to each other and without a word started to run back down the hill, out of the woods and towards the car. The young cat turned to watch them. As soon as he understood that they were about to leave him where he stood, he started down the hill after them. He saw the car edge out into the road and he stopped as he saw it drive off. He gazed after it, his large flecked amber eyes unblinking, as he stood quite still. After some moments he opened his mouth and let out an anguished howl, at first tentatively and then with increased intensity as his utter loneliness overwhelmed him.

Kirstie, still hidden behind her tree, covered her mouth in dismay as he wailed out. She wasn't the only one to hear him. The little wood mouse heard him. The vigilant rooks heard him. A solitary blackbird heard him. A three-quarters-grown rabbit heard him and a small bank vole heard him. A new predator had been added to the woodland register.

White Chin sat down amongst the leaves, looking down the length of the empty road, bewildered and sad. A bank of clouds scudded across the sun and the late afternoon breeze blew with a chill bite. His tremble turned into a violent shiver.

In his whole life he had never strayed beyond the yard of the terraced house where he'd been born, surrounded by the sound of noisy city traffic. As to catching food for himself, he didn't have the first idea. In recent weeks he had started to investigate any small life that moved around him, and spiders in particular interested him since he had discovered they were good to eat. One day, by accident, he had jumped on and killed a young bluetit who was hanging on the bird feeder, but he hadn't eaten the bird because the feathers made him sneeze.

Now, finding himself surrounded by these great dark looming trees he felt a bit frightened. And lonely. For a start there was no sound of traffic and apart from a trace of the grey car there was no smell of oil or petrol in the air. The smells and sounds of the wood and its wildlife were totally new to him. He could hear a great mixture of bird, insect and animal sounds but he had no idea what sort of creatures might be making these noises. White Chin had no experience to draw on, only instinct.

Hungry and thirsty, he turned around and climbed back up the hill to investigate the wood. As he did so, he saw a young girl coming down towards him. She called out to him, but he ran away. He was not used to strangers and he was unaccustomed to being out in the open air. Whilst he longed to be looked after and cuddled, he was confused by all the things that had happened to him and keeping still and hidden felt like the safest thing to do. He didn't know who this girl was or what she wanted with him.

Kirstie called out again, but White Chin stayed crouched beneath a fern. The little girl called one more time. Nothing. Shrugging sadly, she wandered off down the hill, swinging the basket of nuts she had collected before the grey car approaching High Fell Wood had disturbed her.

When White Chin was sure she had gone, he crept out. He nibbled at some grass but it soon made him feel sick. He wandered off and found a pool of water in a hollow stone, which he lapped at for a long time, raising his head at every strange sound. Some leaves rasped together, making him jump. Twice his body tensed in alarm as he heard falling leaves and small twigs cracking underfoot. This wood was a noisy place.

At last the little cat's luck changed. He saw and pounced upon a large spider which he hastily gobbled up. Sitting down after his snack, he licked his lips, then cleaned his whiskers and buffed his ears with each forepaw in turn, like the well brought-up cat that he was.

White Chin looked around him. He still felt hungry. He really would have to find something else to eat, and soon.

# 2

## Told-you-so! Told-you-so! Told-you-so!

As White Chin went deeper into the wood the snapping noises increased and his fear made the blood thump loudly in his ears. He could see daylight showing through the trees to his right so he climbed the hill towards it.

After a while he found himself in a clearing that contained a large expanse of grass and several mounds of dark, freshly dug soil. White Chin stopped and settled down in the low evening sun close to one of the mounds. Suddenly the earth next to him moved. He tensed and sniffed at the soil. It moved again. He could hear and feel digging below. White Chin watched the ground intently, his ears revolving to pick up every sound. Experimentally he patted the top of the soil with his right paw. He was nervous. He didn't know what to expect. The soil moved again. The little cat pulled back and licked his nose in fear.

Suddenly what looked like two large pink hands ending in long dirty fingernails exploded through the soil. These were immediately followed by a pink snout sporting fine whiskers and an enormous black velvety head.

The near-sightless mole, who was rising from the earth with such energy, paused and for one second seemed to float above the ground. The scent of cat was inflaming his nostrils, and with a wisdom learned from several near misses, he quickly sank back again into the safety of his underworld. When he reached a comfortable depth he shuffled in the direction of his main tunnel and from there to one of the small chambers off it, where he kept his food. It was here, in this grim larder, that he stored his giant horde of worms. Like most moles he had learned the trick of biting into the head of each worm as he met one, which kept the creature alive and fresh but unable to move. A rapid snack of worm was enough to reassure him that all was well.

Back above ground White Chin, having missed his first chance to catch this strange animal with the strong earthy whiff, hunched forward again to have another look and poked enquiringly with his right paw into the soil, but the mole smell had weakened and he lost interest. Sitting down again, he opened his jaws wide in a dislocating cat yawn revealing prominent fangs. Every inch of this small animal was evolved as a perfect killing machine and his teeth were impeccably designed to cut, scrape and tear the flesh he might expect to kill in the wild.

White Chin stood up and scented the air. His ears flicked and semi-rotated to collect any and every sound that might mean food or danger, or something interesting to play with. Preparing himself for action, he stretched out his body to its fullest length. He pushed out his front legs first, as far as they would go, bottom high in the air. Then he leaned forward pushing his shoulders high, and drew out each of his back legs in turn, shaking them free of some imaginary wetness. That done, he bounded up the bank to the highest vantage point he could find.

He sniffed around the base of the trunks amongst the banks of leaves gathered beneath them. He looked up to catch a glimpse of the birds that were more audible than visible in the crowns of the trees far above him. The birds were already starting their farewell hymn to the day. White Chin watched the little robin singing his wistful autumn song from on high. Its piercing tones hurt his ears and he turned his back on it, knowing the bird to be beyond his reach. An invisible blackbird now started up with his own sweet tune, which was soon joined by a song thrush, singing 'told-you-so, told-you-so, told-you-so' firmly.

The cat lowered his sights. He stared closely at a clump of bushes from which he had smelt a strange odour – slightly mouse-like, but stronger. His excitement had built up as he heard a series of brief high-pitched squeaks that suddenly stopped.

In the first five months of the little cat's life all the food he had eaten had been dried or cooked. Now, however, with an empty belly, he *knew* that what he could hear and smell was a possible meal and he froze into attentive stillness. The small shrew who crept innocently closer was, like the mole, another eager worm-eater born with bad eyesight but superb senses of hearing and smell. Using these skills she was currently concentrating all her energies on digging in the soft earth beneath her for a long earthworm who was burrowing noisily in White Chin's direction.

White Chin's muscles locked and his breathing almost stopped as he concentrated all his attention on this dark-furred pointy-nosed mammal. When the shrew was nearly upon him, he sprang forward and grabbed her by the back of her neck. The shrew let out one shrill squeak of fear as the cat's canine teeth cut through her spinal cord. She struggled briefly and then went limp in his mouth. White Chin had killed his first shrew and it was well that it had been done quickly. White Chin was yet to discover, as he would later on, that pound for pound of bodyweight, shrews are the most fearless warriors around when fighting for their lives. He let out a high-pitched, almost feminine miaow in triumph. In some haste he devoured the shrew, glancing around him nervously to make sure that no one was about to take his prey from him.

He had nearly finished his little meal, when suddenly he stopped. The taste in his mouth was no longer good. He had swallowed the bitter juices that shrews produce in their glands. Now he needed to find somewhere dark and quiet to hide. He found a large bush which he backed under and there he crouched down, staring out miserably. After a few seconds he was quietly sick. He mewed sadly to himself. Soon, however, he felt a little better and started on a long grooming session. As always he paid particular attention to his whiskers and ears and then, hearing the sound of babbling water in the distance, he slowly clambered through the leaves in its direction.

Dusk was falling and the daytime songbirds were taking their last feed before going to their roosts in hedge and tree. Those who had already fed were singing their own individual songs announcing their possession of territory and warning all others to keep clear. It was that moment in the evening when, as the birds of darkness wake up and start their hunting calls to each other, there is a brief noisy overlap of the two worlds. A tawny owl, who had hunted in silence through most of the summer, started his penetrating low call of autumn, with his special, teasingly long pause, as if he was taking an enormous breath before the final 'Tut-whoooh':

'Whoooh' . . . 'Tut-whoooh' . . . 'Whoooh' . . . . . .
'Tut-whoooh'

And all the while the blackbird cock whose patch this was, who had earlier eaten his fill of berries from the yew tree and snowberry bushes, sang his loud flute-like solo from his traditional song-post before starting a somewhat raucous warning 'dik-dik-dik . . . dik-dik-dik'.

White Chin had passed the blackbird's song-post without the slightest intention of disturbing him, and was surprised at the violence of the bird's alarm call. It made the little cat hurry by to get away from it. White Chin was to become familiar with that call and as he learned of its telltale nature he liked it less and less.

Darkness fell and the noises of the woodland changed. It was drizzling steadily and a strong breeze had got up. White Chin could see well enough, but he was sensitive to the changes around him in the gathering night. He had recovered from his reaction to eating the shrew and was now even hungrier than before. The sounds around him worried him less than when he was first abandoned, but he was tense and alert all the same.

The owl cock passed closely over him and as he did so he made one great shrieking 'whooooooooooooo' to his mate, who replied demurely with 'kewick', 'kewick', 'kewick'.

White Chin had never been as close as this to an owl and was slightly alarmed by the huge spread of the bird's wings and its loud cries, but instinct told him he was safe.

The small cat now discovered an unexpected benefit of following in the wake of this great aerial hunter. A small wood mouse scuttled off into the bushes close by, followed quickly by two more. White Chin went after them and sat very quietly by the thicket where they had disappeared. His patience was rewarded as a small male wood mouse ventured out to be caught immediately by the cat, who having killed his prey, sniffed and licked the tiny body thoroughly, checking for any sign of that bad musty smell he had encountered on the shrew. His mouse smelt good and White Chin ate again, crunchily, and this time his meal stayed in his belly. Soon all that remained visible of the mouse were a few teeth, a couple of feet and a tail.

The rain started to penetrate the outer layer of White Chin's fur and made him shiver. The little cat found a small sheltered patch of ground under a tree and there he set about licking himself dry. Leaves blew around in the wind, and being a cat, he started to pounce on them, pretending to kill them fiercely, ripping and clawing them into little bits. Now he had eaten he felt bouncy and wanted to play, but it was boring on his own. He wanted company. He wanted his mother and everyone else back in the house in the city. This dark wood, where he had been so cruelly tossed away, was lonely and wet and scary.

As he sat there he heard a distant barking sound. To

begin with it sounded like a dog – there had been dogs near his home in the city – but as he listened it changed. It became more like a screech, like a human, but then it lowered to a bark again. White Chin had heard his first fox. He trembled without knowing why. It sounded a long way off, but he wanted to find somewhere safer than here. Slinking in short spurts, low to the ground, he ran away from the sounds of barking and screeching, although as he paused and listened they didn't come any closer. After running some distance, he found himself getting deeper into the dark wood. Might those tree roots provide some shelter?

The little cat started frantically scratching and sniffing. His nose and ears told him there was an empty space in front of him. Then, as he pawed aside another pile of dead leaves, he uncovered the entrance to a small cave. It was formed out of limestone rocks and covered in moss, hidden by the leaves of several autumns banked up against the entrance. It was difficult to crawl into it; he had to squeeze right down with his bottom sticking out in the air, but when he did get into it he was happy to find that it went back a long way and it was dry. Other animals had used it and left their scents behind, but for the moment at least it appeared to be empty.

White Chin tucked himself into the very back of the cave, pulling together a bed of dried-up leaves with his paw. He started to turn in little circles to make a hollow in the centre. Satisfied at last that his bed was as it should be, he curled into a ball. As he slept, his tail twitched. He was dreaming of mice and his mouth curved from the pleasure of it.

# 3

# The music of the night

Through the night White Chin was woken by an assortment of noises. In spite of these disturbances he remained curled up until a loud huffing sound came so close that he feared it would come right into his cave. At this he got up and thrust his head out through the opening to judge whether he should make a quick run for it.

What he saw, immediately outside, was a large round-backed hedgehog using his long pointy nose to sniff out beetles in a snorty hedgehoggy kind of way. White Chin had no idea what he was looking at. They briefly held each other's gaze and then released each other by looking away again. The hedgehog resumed his rootling. He was having his last feast of the year before he retired into hibernation, and he wasn't going to let anyone put him off! He had no fear of White Chin, nor White Chin of him. The little cat crawled back to the inner peace of his cave, turned around and curled up again.

On and off for the rest of the night he heard an assortment of cries and squeaks from the woodland around him, but they rarely caused him to do more than open an eye and settle back down to sleep. The emotional strain of being away from the comforts of home, an ongoing fear of his current surroundings and his recurring concern about the hunger he felt had left him exhausted. Sleep made all these things disappear. The rain continued through the night, and sometimes the heavy bursts woke him and he lay there listening to it. It sounded much wetter and noisier than when he had lived in a house. If he had but known it, he was fortunate to have found a sleeping place that remained dry on this soaking wet autumn night and as the splashing shafts of water slowed down to a drizzle and then fell as steady rain again, he felt warm enough to tuck his nose under his front leg and fall into a deep sleep.

At one point he awoke and found he was sharing his new quarters with a rodent unlike any he had yet met. He was being studied by a small brown mammal with a snub nose, long whiskers, glittering eyes and round ears. The bank vole stared in horror at him and once she realised he was looking back at her she skittered away down a tiny tunnel into her burrow below, where, like the wood mouse, she was building up her store of nuts for the winter months. As she moved along her burrow she squeaked repeatedly in alarm. Immediately following this encounter White Chin was kept awake for some time, while the bank vole shuffled back and forth in her nearby tunnel, scratchily ramming acorns at the junction where her hole met White Chin's cave. She was building herself a fortress. White Chin crawled over to inspect the work in progress. He yawned and turned around to sleep, unmoved by the little vole's exertions. She was safe from him, without all her effort. He would never have fitted into her burrow. At last the vole's entrance was sealed to her satisfaction and she fell silent, secure now in her fastness. White Chin continued snoring gently.

Beyond the woods, lower down the valley, at the far side of the village, Kirstie lay in her farmhouse bed, wide awake. Her head was filled with thoughts of the little black-and-white cat she had watched being dumped in High Fell Wood. Earlier in the evening she had heard foxes barking and wondered whether White Chin was all right up there on his own. She imagined him being frightened and hungry. She thought about the men who had left him there. Would they be able to sleep calmly in their beds back in the big town they had come from, knowing that the little cat was roaming the wet wild woods? What sort of home had he been in? Had there been children who had loved him and who would, even now, be crying at his loss? Did they think he had gone to a new and loving home?

She was restless and getting out of bed she crossed to the window. The darkness was oddly unyielding and she couldn't see anything other than her own reflection. Raindrops played races with each other down the windowpane, joining others and getting so big they burst with their own weight to form tiny channels of water that ran down the glass and disappeared over the windowsill. Her breath formed a mist on the glass and so, with her finger, she drew a little cat. She shivered and climbed back into her warm bed. She resolved that she would ride out on her Fell pony, Buster, and look for him as soon as ever she could.

Up in High Fell Wood the tawny owls, who had called through most of the night, increased the frequency of their hunting cries to each other around first light, just as the woodland birds stuttered out the first bars of their dawn chorus. By this time White Chin had had enough of the rowdy animals of the night and left the shelter of his cave to tour his new territory. The rain had stopped and the sun was rising, yet the air remained cool.

Although the young cat had had good fortune yesterday evening with his mouse supper, the new dawn offered no sign of any meal. He crept down to the stream and scented other mammals that had passed that way. He could smell rabbit, something he hadn't encountered in the flesh, but it excited him nonetheless. He could tell that wood mice and bank voles had passed this way recently, but strongest of all the scents was the rank odour left on the grasses of the bank by a shrew who had scurried past only seconds earlier. It was a smell he would now remember forever. He stepped forward and played at paw-catching the trickling water before lapping at it for some minutes. He jumped across the stream, which had so far been one of his boundaries, and started to explore. As the little black cat with the showy white bib, uneven white socks and wonky white chin wandered slowly through the wood, a solitary crow surveyed him from on high. The bird shouted out in a deep rasping voice for everyone to hear,

'Craaaar, craaaar, craaaar, craaaar.'

Although the cat's ears flipped back and forth, he quickly ceased paying attention to the carrion crow as his senses became focussed entirely on the ground in front of him, unaware that this dark sentry was announcing his presence to the entire woodland. He disturbed a log as he jumped on it. It rolled over revealing a small beetle and a long worm that had been sheltering beneath. Without hesitating the cat gobbled both up. He had no difficulty with the beetle, which disappeared down his throat in a matter of seconds. The worm, on the other hand, he found very chewy, but eventually, with a mighty gulp, he got it down.

White Chin ventured deeper into the wood than he had yet been, climbing up a tree-clad hill, until he reached a small grassy clearing lit by dappled sunlight. At the base of a giant oak tree there was a series of large holes in the bank, with an arch of roots providing a ceiling to the entrance of an imposing tunnel. A network of small roots was hanging down over the cavernous hole, like a small curtain. On the ground, some distance from the front of the entrance, was a pile of what looked like discarded bedding and large drag marks in the soil. As White Chin scented the air around him, he was aware of a musky stench unlike anything he had ever encountered before. It was strong and floated up in powerful wafts from within the deep cavern that stretched away in front of him. Instinct made him wary, but he didn't feel afraid. He examined every inch of the wide path leading up to the biggest entrance. Then he stopped. Someone was in there!

Although the timid part of him made him want to rush away from the cave and continue his search for food elsewhere, some other part of his brain made him hang around the entrance to the cave. He rolled over on his back and scent-marked the soil around the entrance. Having done this he was about to walk away when, for good measure, he decided to spray the tree closest to the entrance. Some basic instinct was making him announce he was there, and that he was one tough cat.

Just as he completed this bold act, something terrible happened! Out of the cave came a deep, rumbling growl. It lasted only a few seconds, but it made every hair on White Chin's body stand out in alarm, making him look like a black-and-white bottle brush. He jumped to one side – all four feet off the ground – with his back arched like the round of a full moon. As his feet touched down he raced away as fast as a cat can run. He had no idea what lay within that cave, but his senses told him that something that could make so deep and terrifying a sound must be gigantic. As the little cat galloped through the trees he imagined an enormous snarling monster gnashing angry teeth close behind him, about to grab him by his tail.

White Chin ran without ceasing until, at last, he could see the rolling fields beyond the forest. He felt safer here, although there were fewer places to hide; there were fewer places for others to hide as well. As he reached a low drystone wall, he jumped on top of it and stopped to listen. His heart was beating fast from his long gallop, but slowly he breathed deeply and the blood stopped banging in his ears. He paused, checked behind and sprang down the far side of the wall, hiding himself amidst a group of tall rushes. The little cat was in need of some quiet. He found a dry hollow in the long grasses and sank down out of sight.

Time passed and White Chin dozed. He awoke, all attention, having heard a slight scratching sound across a stony patch of ground. The smell, which was coming closer and closer, was new to him. He stood up to see a long bronze-coloured reptile snaking towards him. She had scales on her body and as the cat watched her he saw her blink her eye. As the reptile wound her way in his direction, her notched tongue flickered in and out tasting the air. Her favourite food was slugs and worms and that was how she hunted them down. White Chin waited and then, as the creature drew close to him, he pounced. The reptile curled round, unexpectedly muscled and strong. White Chin released her and grabbed again, feeling her pulling with all her strength as she writhed from side to side. Then, suddenly, he was left with a wriggling tail under his front feet as he heard the rest of the reptile slither away at great speed into the grass behind him. White Chin looked down in surprise finding he was holding a still twitching tail which the female slow-worm had shed in order to save her own life. Although this legless lizard would never regain her former full-tailed glory, she had at least survived this attack.

White Chin licked the trophy tail between his front paws, but found it didn't amount to much and, when it finally stopped writhing, left it lying on the ground like a dead thing. He remained hungry and for a while he dug around in the grass until he found a worm, which he ate from necessity, with little pleasure. Worms were rubbery and cold. He changed his mind and went back to the slow-worm tail. He threw it around trying to make it wriggle again, but it wouldn't play with him any more. He held it down with one paw, just in case, and crunched his way through it noisily. It was different from worms, but he wasn't sure it was any better.

## 4

# Know thine enemy

As the weeks passed, White Chin began to understand better the world of the wood and its many noises and smells. His hunting reactions had sharpened. He had learned to be patient when watching for small mammals.

Worm, certainly while the weather was wet, was the easiest to find but the least satisfying. Wood mouse on the other hand was harder to capture but had the best flavour and was wonderfully crunchy. The chase itself was everything, and the little cat was getting better at it day upon day. Whenever he killed a mouse now he ate every scrap of it, scrunching up the bones and chewing through the fur-covered skin without fear. Sometimes he even ate the teeth, tail and feet – everything. He had caught and killed two birds, but adult birds, which were all that he could find, seemed sharply aware of him and ever watchful. The warning sound of the blackbird, the harsh repetitive 'dik-dik-dik', 'dik-dik-dik' alerted not only birds but mammals also to his presence and as soon as he heard the sneaky alarm calls he would move out of sight of these bouncing black monitors. Stomach pains had taught him what carrion was fit to eat and what not, but he preferred his meat fresh. He would even eat frogs and fish as well when he could find them.

In the long weeks that White Chin spent in the wet wild woods, as the warm wet autumn cooled into winter, he learned that cats have enemies and these came in many different forms. He now knew that sneaky low-slung stoats and weasels were to be avoided – they had sharp teeth, ran very fast and couldn't be trusted – and that great brown-backed buzzards with giant wings, yellow claws and cruel beaks could make an attack on any earthbound creature in complete silence. He had had an alarmingly close encounter with one such sky raider. The little cat had been quietly sitting close to a bank vole nest, when he felt the whoosh of air from under the wings of a hawk as it turned up into the sky away from him. The buzzard had thought that he was a rabbit and changed his mind at the very last second before attacking with his killer claws. The scare taught White Chin not to ignore the skies in future. From that time on, whenever he heard the sharp mewing 'kiew' of a buzzard echoing around the surrounding hills, he kept well hidden.

The cat yearned to catch a rabbit himself but, try though he might, he failed every time. Each time he had got within range of a group of rabbits the one on sentry duty had done loud warning thumps with its back legs and off they all ran – and they could gallop! All he ever saw was a host of white cotton-tails disappearing into the distance. He encountered, too, the tall roe deer who lived all year round in High Fell Wood. They moved around in couples or family groups, but he learned very quickly that they were not interested in him. They were timid, fast-moving creatures, and White Chin soon understood they would run from him, rather than cause him any harm. He hadn't yet met any foxes, although sometimes he heard them barking and he had picked up their scent markings. He had no desire to meet one, but he liked to check on their whereabouts.

Several times he had seen Kirstie riding through the woods on her dark brown Fell pony, Buster, but the horse had scared him. He had never seen anything so huge, with its great black hairy mane and furry legs. White Chin, who now understood how to become invisible, had melted away into the trees as soon as the hoof beats came close.

One morning he was peering intently into a bramble bush, where he had picked up the scent of wood mouse, when he heard the thudding of Buster's hooves on the hard woodland floor behind him. For once, White Chin didn't run away but held his hunting position as he reckoned he was about to get his mouse, and the horse got closer.

Suddenly there was a loud human shout as the pony jumped to one side in alarm at a blackbird who had shot across right under his feet. This was followed by the loud thud of his rider hitting the ground. The riderless pony trotted on a few yards, empty stirrups banging his sides and then, never one to miss an opportunity, he stopped and put his head down to graze. White Chin, whose mouse had now escaped, looked across at the fallen body. It was Kirstie and she was lying flat on her back with her arms and legs out like an upside-down frog, struggling to get her breath. Slowly she turned over and her eyes met White Chin's. The cat scented her delight as she spied him.

'Hey, White Chin. Promise not to tell! I'm s'posed to stay on top of him, not lie under him!' She crouched up on her knees and laughed happily, putting her hand out.

'Oh hey, come here, come on. Puss, puss, puss.' Slowly, very slowly, White Chin edged towards her. She placed her fingers gently on his head and back and bit by bit she stroked his ears and under his chin. It felt good. He started to purr, looking up into her eyes. They stayed like that for a while and as her fingers stroked him repeatedly White Chin licked the back of her hand with his rough rasping tongue. Kirstie, remembering that she had to seek out the wayward Buster, jumped to her feet, and the spell was broken. White Chin slunk away into the woods.

From this time on, more often than not, White Chin would meet Kirstie rather than melt away between the trees. The cat enjoyed the presence of the girl, and loved her to talk to him, which she would do for minutes on end. But still he avoided letting her pick him up. People were not to be trusted. All these long weeks White Chin had felt unloved and missed human friendship, but his instinct for survival made him cautious of being hurt again. He had a strong sense now that having been abandoned in these woods, he had been mistreated. People did bad things to cats.

White Chin, who had now become a true hunter, began to mark out a familiar territory within the wood that had become his world. His scent was prominent throughout the wood and he was now at ease in it, day or night. When he wanted to sleep, either for the colder parts of the night or during heavy rain, he returned to the little moss-covered cave he had found on his first night. He still shared this with the reluctant bank vole, who continued to live in a state of anxiety in her parallel tunnel.

White Chin was changing and beginning to feel braver in this wild world, although he rarely felt safe enough to completely relax. His hunting skills continued to improve, but he had forgotten what it was like to have a full belly. Sometimes, after he had squeezed himself into his cave, he would look out of the entrance with distant eyes, almost happy, but still aching for something just out of reach.

One afternoon, following a violent shower, White Chin dozed in the shelter of a stone wall, warmed by the slanting rays of the winter sun. His tail twitched as he slept and he made funny snorting sounds as he dreamt. He was in a deep dark cave, and there was a strong pong coming from a long tunnel and loud deep snarls were getting closer and closer. As he dozed, a ragged-winged ginger and black butterfly, a Comma about to start her big winter sleep, landed on his nose and the fussy trembling of her wings woke him with a start.

White Chin rose, yawning widely, stretched and sprang lightly over the wall leading back into the woods. He padded up the hill between avenues of trees, waving his long tail in and out of a question mark as he moved. As he entered deeper into the wood the long shafts of sunlight lit up the raindrops clinging to the undergrowth so that they glittered like tiny jewels. White Chin was on a mission. Who was that big beast? Why did he growl so? What was in that big black cave that he was protecting? Might there be something good to eat in there?

In all his wanderings over the many days he had

been alone the little cat had avoided the cavern in the high wood. He had thought often about that deep growl and the powerful smell that came from inside the cave was sharp in his memory. Now he would find out.

White Chin retraced his steps towards the giant cavern. As he approached he moved more slowly. He came to a halt and stood to one side, scenting the air and watching quietly. There wasn't a sound although that rank musk smell was everywhere. This time White Chin had the good manners not to scent mark the area and after a suitable lapse of time he cautiously approached the entrance to the large burrow. Nothing happened. No one came. There wasn't a sound to be heard. The cat crept forward. He went deeper as the passage started to slope downwards. The other animal smell was overpowering now. And then, as White Chin's eyes became accustomed to the gloom, at last he saw the creature in whose domain he now dared to stand.

A large mammal, twice the size of the little cat, stood facing him, swaying slightly and grunting menacingly. White Chin could make out a black chest and black forepaws topped by a huge black-and-white striped head with round white-tipped ears. The black mud-covered nose was moving rapidly from side to side and the beast's large scarred muzzle was wrinkled up in concentration, while he absorbed by scent and hearing everything he could about White Chin; who he was and what he might be about.

White Chin was staring straight up into the shortsighted eyes of an old badger boar, who, having been so rudely awoken from his customary daytime sleep by this young upstart, was very grumpy indeed. The old badger was the undisputed master of the clan that occupied the largest badger sett this side of the fell and he was in no mood for any nonsense.

He growled at the cat. It was a brief but terrifying noise. He rumbled again, more threateningly.

White Chin licked his nose nervously but stood his ground in silence. He felt small and wished he hadn't come. He longed to hiss defensively, but instinct told him it would be unwise. After what seemed to White Chin like for ever, he decided it would be all right if he started, most politely and gently, to back out the full length of the cave. The badger followed him for a short distance, swaying his head back and forth, making belchy, cross noises, determined that this tiresome cat would continue on his journey, never to return.

As White Chin emerged from the cave, he took great gulps of the sweet fresh air. He licked his nose and then started to walk forward casually as if he had never been worried at all. Suddenly he stopped in his tracks. He had scented the badger smell again, ahead of him and up to his left. He nervously turned his head in its direction. There was a round hole further along the bank, which White Chin now realised was another entrance to the sett and to his dismay he saw the badger he had so recently parted from standing there watching him, filling the opening with his bulk.

The big boar stood grunting at the small tomcat and then he pushed his head forward, swaying, and growled deeply. The message was unmistakable.

Go away and stay away. Or else!

White Chin knew that he should put as much distance as possible between himself and the badger he had so unwisely disturbed and he started to move through the woods with purpose. The freshness of the air around him after the heavy musk of the badger underworld was pure joy and he breathed it in, in great hungry gulps.

The little cat trotted towards the woodland haunts where he felt at home, towards his familiar sleeping cave and as he did so the badger sett was left far behind him. But the memory of it would remain with him always. It was a lesson learned: messing with badgers was a bad idea.

## 5

## Blow, blow, thou winter wind

As autumn became winter the weather worsened and White Chin found it increasingly difficult to catch food. The wind had been thrashing through the woods for some days, but now it veered around to the north-west and rain started to blow in icy flurries.

The air felt different and the trees swayed and bent as the wind rose up in blustery gusts. In all the weeks that the little cat had so bravely survived in the woods, he had never seen the trees moving around in this way, or heard the wind sound so angry. This was different from anything he had known. It howled and screamed and even when there was a quieter spell, it still moaned in the background. The smaller trees and bushes whipped down and round and about, brushing the ground as if they would tear themselves out of it and run away. White Chin wanted to run with them. He was aware of the woodland birds behaving erratically too, as they were buffeted from one roost to another as the wind hurled itself around the branches of the trees. The rooks and jays called out their warnings to each other in rasping tones as they flounced up over the trees and flew away out of trouble. Over the sound of the mighty wind great rolling claps of thunder could be heard, followed by torrential rain. The air was exploding with the sounds of a storm in full spate.

White Chin wanted to get out of this threatening wood. He ran up into the highest part of it, and out into the open where he hid in a hedgerow, away from the trees. The wind still roared but without the complaining trees it was quieter. Above the whooshing wind he could hear the rattling of a small engine and a dog barking excitedly. White Chin shrank back into the hedgerow, wanting not to be seen. He had no time for dogs.

'Dad, Dad – the sheep are OVER THERE, quick!' Kirstie was jumping up and down in the trailer at the back of her father's quad bike, frantically holding on to the hood of her Peter Storm jacket, pointing away from the direction he was driving. She was laughing into the wind and her hair was blowing wildly around her.

John Metcalfe stopped and turned the bike in the direction she was pointing. He whistled Shep into action. The Border Collie leapt out of the trailer and now, all seriousness, he raced, low-bellied and obedient, after the Rough Fell sheep.

Kirstie also clambered from the quad bike and wandered off to look for the little cat. The man and the dog worked together herding the sheep into an orderly group, before John jumped back onto his quad bike to drive them as a flock by way of the road down into a lower, sheltered pasture. As the man, dog and sheep progressed down the road, Kirstie could hear her father's shrill whistlings periodically interrupted by his mild curses as Shep interpreted an instruction in his own way and a wayward sheep broke ranks. Sometimes the sound of John's laughter would drift up as he praised his dog for working the sheep well in spite of everything.

Kirstie remained on the high fell, calling out repeatedly for White Chin. As she called for him her brows furrowed with concern. Often at night, as she lay in her warm bed, she thought about White Chin up here on his own. This little black-and-white cat had touched her heart in a special way and she longed for him to come home with her and let her love him. There was a terrible storm forecast and she desperately hoped that their frequent meetings might now lead him to trust her.

'White Chin, come on, White Chin, where are you?' Suddenly she saw a flash of white as the little cat lifted his head and his chin and chest became visible. She started to walk slowly towards the hedge holding out her hand in a cajoling way. Another clap of thunder rumbled loudly and long, followed by three sharp flashes of lightning. White Chin shrank further back and out of her reach.

Kirstie got down on her knees in the mud and whispered, 'Come on, little cat, I won't hurt you. I promise . . . Come home with me, to safety.' She saw a pair of dark amber eyes with large frightened pupils staring back at her, barely blinking. His ears were flat and his whiskers pointed down. He licked his black nose with a very pink tongue. She smiled and put her hand out towards him.

At that moment White Chin did indeed want to trust this little girl, whom he had come to know and whose voice was so gentle. He stood up and started to go towards her, but suddenly the wind gusted up again and whistled loudly along the hedge bottom and a rook cawed a harsh warning sound. The little cat lowered his gaze, flattened himself and crawled backwards, out of her sight. Kirstie turned round as she heard the rattling of the quad bike and her father's shout.

'Come on, Kirstie-girl, we've work to do and animals to feed and it'll be dark soon.'

'But Dad, that little cat I told you about is here! In this hedge somewhere. We can't leave him – please?'

Kirstie wailed out against the noise of the wind. She held her hands together and her eyes pleaded with those of her father. John Metcalfe looked down at his daughter and sighed.

He heaved himself up off his bike, and tousled her hair. Together, on foot, father and daughter thoroughly searched the hedgerow and the border of the fell pasture, accompanied by a few encouraging yaps from Shep, who was promptly sent back to the quad bike to sit and wait. After searching for more than a quarter of an hour John reached down for Kirstie's hand and gave it a squeeze.

'It's no good, lass. We're going to have to call it a day. He could be anywhere on the fell by now.'

Kirstie looked up at her father in anguish.

'Oh Dad, I don't see how he can survive out here on his own in this storm. It's vile weather. We've just GOT to find him.' John shrugged and started to make his way back to the quad bike. Kirstie ran after him and as she caught up with him she pummelled his back with both her fists, yelling and crying in frustration. John stopped and swung around, catching her hands in his.

'Kirstie, that's quite enough!' he said, firmly. 'Calm down, now! Animals are tough, as you well know. He'll find himself shelter. There's houses and barns in the village. He'll be all right.' He put his hand on her shoulder and guided her to the bike, where Shep awaited them.

'Listen, that cat's already coped with some pretty

foul conditions. And he looks all right, you tell me. So he's done OK till now, has your little cat, hasn't he?' John asked, gently. Kirstie wrinkled her freckled nose and pulled a face. Reluctantly she nodded her head. The farmer grinned and started the engine. With a heavy heart Kirstie clambered up into the small open sheep trailer. She gripped the iron standing bar fiercely. They rattled off down the hill and as the cold wind blew into her face, her eyes filled with tears.

White Chin, meanwhile, had taken one look at the sheepdog and decided that going back into the trees was his safest option. By the time the quad bike had left the high fell White Chin was deep inside the woods.

The frightened little cat was unsure where he was going, but he knew he must find shelter. The wind from the storm was screaming like a wild thing and all around him he could hear the creaking and moaning of trees; trees that had grown from saplings to full maturity through many an autumn gale in the past, but for whom this particular wind was to be their slayer. Two young silver birches had already been wrenched from their moorings and were lying at strange drunken angles against other trees with their roots suspended in mid-air, still dangling clods of earth.

The little cat passed a large tree with low branches sweeping right down to the ground that had black warty-looking buds at their tips. They were tossing and swaying around and, as he passed, they caught at him like huge witches' claws. As White Chin dodged out of the way of the grasping talons, the giant swaying ash tree, for this it was, cracked with an ear-splitting sound, trembled and made a mighty groan, as if in pain. A weakened joint in its main trunk, caused by frost when it was a sapling more than seventy years earlier, split noisily apart from the main trunk and, slowly, creakingly, half the tree started to fall to the ground, crushing and ripping through other trees and bushes as it came. It thudded to earth where the little cat had stood moments earlier.

White Chin felt the pulse of fear pound in his head. He quivered, shaking under a clump of bushes and miaowed pitifully. His mewlings were swallowed up by the great throaty roar of the storm. The rain was pouring down in what seemed like solid slanting lines, and when they hit the cat, they were stingingly painful. Enough was enough.

White Chin had been going to return to his usual little cave, but now the wood had become too terrifying a place to stay. He wanted to get out of it. He wanted to go far away. He wanted to go home. With a supreme effort he got up, shook the excess water off his dripping back, and ran in short, zig-zaggy spurts through the trees. It took him a long time to get across the wood as there were so many obstacles in his way and he had to use all his strength to move against the wild winds and not get hopelessly blown off course. Eventually the trees started to thin and he found the downhill track for which he had been looking. He climbed down the path and came to a large iron gate. He had never ventured further than this gate before but now, flattening his legs frog-like, he squeezed underneath it to find himself standing on a long grassy track that led to a road at the bottom.

As he started his descent he became aware of a large stone house on the left, surrounded by trees and bushes and a long low stone wall. A light was shining out into the wet blackness from one of the downstairs windows. White Chin stood for some moments in the dark night as the rain trickled round his ears and down his back and then he seemed to make up his mind. The little cat's ears pricked forward and he put up his tail as he walked towards the light.

## 6

## Butter wouldn't melt

White Chin scrambled under an iron gate in the stone wall and found himself in a large garden. He had entered the grounds of Fellside House. As he neared the front door a light came on, dazzling him. He stood still, but nothing happened. He crept forward and examined the smells around the front door. They told him that this was where people came and went. There was no scent of any animals; just people. He peered up at the glass door but he couldn't see through it. There was a huge curtain in the way. He looked back at where the light was shining out into the garden. It was coming from a window with bushes in front of it. He stood up and put his front feet on a little ledge.

White Chin found himself looking into a deeply carpeted room with two sofas at angles to each other. A woman was sitting on one of them reading a book and on the other a man was hunched forward, watching a large flickering screen. The sofas were drawn up in front of a wide hearth containing massive logs that blazed cheerily up the chimney. The firelight was making shadows dance across the walls and ceiling. The little cat stared through the window with a profound sense of yearning. He miaowed. No one in the room moved and the sensor light went out. White Chin jumped down. He looked behind him at the garden being buffeted by the wind and rain. Remounting the window ledge, he miaowed again. The sensor light came back on.

Anna put down her book. She walked across the room, shading her eyes and peered out into the garden.

'I could have sworn I heard a cat a few minutes ago and that blasted security light keeps going on and off,' she complained to her husband. She continued to stand at the window.

'Stuart, Stuart, come here, quick! Look. It *is* a cat!' Stuart rose from the sofa and joined her at the window. White Chin, still standing on his back legs peering into the room, opened his mouth and miaowed silently at them.

'What do you think we should do?' Anna asked.

'Well let the poor little blighter in, I'd say.'

'Oh, but it's soaked through and it'll probably have fleas. Yuck, we can't. Look at it, it's some mangy feral cat.'

As she said this a violent squall of wind made a cloud of smoke gust back down the chimney into the room. A metal dustbin lid clattered noisily along the stone flags at the back of the house and a fresh wave of driving rain battered heavily against the windowpanes. The man touched his wife gently on the arm.

'You can't leave the poor little scrap out in this, come on. It's blowing a helluva gale out there and I'm sure he isn't a feral cat. Wild cats would never peer through a window like that. They would . . . they would . . . ' his voice petered out.

'They would what, Stuart?'

He shrugged. 'Oh you know, they would rather hole up in some barn, or something.'

'Well that cat's not coming in here. Over my dead body!'

Stuart shot a mock stern glance at his wife in response to this ban and then he laughed and touched her arm.

'Come on, girl, where's your heart?' and he started to walk towards the door. Anna groaned as he left the room.

At the front door Stuart drew the curtain to one side and opening it up to the full force of the gale he started to call.

'Kitty, kitty, kitty. Here puss.'

White Chin heard him make that loud sort of kissing noise that people think cats like. He longed to be inside that warm dry house, but it had been many weeks since he had known such comfort and these people were strangers to him. How could he trust them? He crept along the wall of the house and hid around the corner, out of sight.

Stuart knelt down on the doorstep and called again. He disappeared into the kitchen and came back carrying a full saucer of milk, which he put down inside the front door. White Chin, who had crawled forward a little so that he could see what was happening, remained undetected. The coaxing and calling went on for some minutes. Eventually the man stood further back inside the house leaving the front door open a few feet.

Outside White Chin slowly crept closer. His belly was rumbling and he longed to be warm and dry. At last he put one foot, then the other inside the house until he reached the saucer and was able to lap at the milk. Stuart reached forward and quietly shut the door on the storm. As soon as the milk was finished the small cat looked up at the man and then, tail high, he walked into the warm sitting room. Straightaway, he jumped up on the empty sofa, closest to the fire. Anna, seated on the other, watched him, warily.

'Look at the state of that cat. It looks like a drowned rat. Please get it off there at once!'

'Oh don't be such a fusspot, Anna. He won't do any harm and the sofa will dry out in no time.' But Anna had already left the room before he finished speaking and re-entered with a towel with which she fussily attempted to rub White Chin dry. White Chin was appalled. He wriggled and tried to scratch her. He miaowed his protest loudly until she stopped. She grabbed the now wet towel and declaring that she had had more than enough and was going up to bed she walked out of the room.

Now that White Chin was left in peace he was more than happy to just lie on the sofa and watch the fire. He was hypnotised by the flames. The crackling logs were throwing out the first real heat he had felt in weeks and the ferocity of the gale in the woods had really scared him. As he lay there, he slowly started to purr. Stuart came across and scratched him behind his ear and White Chin looked up at him, increasing the revs of his purr. The man smiled at the cat and the cat returned his gaze calmly and then looked away.

Shortly after this Stuart, who had left the room and could be heard banging around in the kitchen, returned with some cut-up slices of cold ham on a piece of kitchen towel. He bent down and gently placed them next to the little cat. White Chin scoffed the food down so fast he was nearly sick. After the last piece had gone he looked up at Stuart with soulful eyes.

'What Oliver, you want some more?' he mocked him. And White Chin would certainly have eaten more if more had been offered to him, but none was. The heat from the fire lulled the little cat into a dreamy slumber and he soon fell deeply asleep, curled up in a tight ball on his chosen sofa.

Later on Stuart stood looking down at the little cat sleeping soundly, and smiling to himself he crept upstairs to join his wife, closing the bedroom door firmly behind him.

The storm continued to blow throughout the night making rattling and banging sounds around the house and the distant roar of the wind could still be heard ripping through the trees in the wood up the lane behind them.

From time to time the little cat would wake up in his new surroundings and listen to the storm raging outside. He would remember, with fear, the violence of the wind when he had been in the wild wood and the way that the very trees seemed to have become his enemies. Then he would blink and look down at the glowing embers of the fire and feel the safety of the house around him and he would yawn, contentedly, and turn around and fall back asleep. He felt safer now than he had for weeks.

As the night wore on and the temperature dropped, the little cat woke up properly. This was the time of night that he would normally go hunting. The time had come to investigate his new surroundings.

White Chin jumped down from his sofa and started

to wander around downstairs. He went in and out of any room that had its door open. He found a room, the shower room, which was completely tiled from floor to ceiling. It contained a drain in a sunken well in the middle of the floor. As soon as he walked in he saw a large spider sitting close to the drainage hole, so without hesitating he jumped on it, flattened it and ate it. He thought the drain was interesting because of the smells coming from it, so he sniffed around it long and hard. After a bit he squatted down and had a wee, adding his own smell to all the others.

He looked around and saw a toilet in the corner with a brown wooden seat. He climbed on the seat and by bracing his back legs he was able to hang down into the bowl and spoon the water up in his paw and then let it run back down again splashily. He had a long drink. Soon he found a big fat roll of pink toilet tissue hanging on a holder. It was wonderful. He was able to spin it round really fast and unravel it. It was very soft and he could rip it into long strips with his claws. He did that until it wouldn't turn any more. As he moved away he had to scuffle through mounds of soft pink paper, which made getting away difficult, and he trailed yards of the stuff after him.

With the joys of the shower room now played out he trotted off down the corridor, tail held high and bent over his back in a jaunty way, until he found the kitchen. Here he smelt food. There were high surfaces but he could not tell what might be on them. White Chin stood up on his back legs to try to see what was there, but it was no good, he couldn't see a thing, so he jumped up to discover the delights that awaited him. As he tiptoed around the top of the units he looked here, sniffed there, and had a little lick at anything that seemed slightly promising. He found a dish with butter in it. It was quite solid so he dug his claws into it and licked his greasy pad. Delicious! He sank his teeth into the top of the block, leaving clear deep tooth grooves.

Leaving the butter, he found a large bowl of white sugar. He dipped in his buttery paw and spooned the sugar into his mouth. It was all right, but a bit sickly. The sugar stuck to his front foot so he had to sit down and lick it all clean. He walked round the other side of the units and found a white paper bag with writing on it. Sniffing it, he was delighted to find that it contained more ham, left out to defrost for breakfast. He tore into the paper with his claws and teeth and ate the rest of the ham until it was all gone. He was beginning to feel full. Hunger satisfied he felt the need for another entertainment.

Once in the dining room, he jumped up on the shiny wooden table. There he found a large cut-glass bowl full of fruit and on the very top of the pile were two pears. He patted the top pear enquiringly and found that if he curved his claws in deeply enough he had just enough strength to support it in mid-air. He held it in the claws of one paw briefly before the weight of it made it bounce across the table and down to the polished wooden floor. White Chin jumped after it and landed on a rag rug, which sledged him across the floor in a rather exciting way the full length of the room, until it got tangled up in a chair leg. He found the pear and clawed it a few more times. Eventually the wounds he had inflicted on the fruit made it impossible to hold any more, because juice was squidging out everywhere and it was turning brown and mushy, so he went back to the fruit bowl and started on the next one until that too stopped behaving like a pear.

White Chin pottered around the house for a little longer, playing with cushion tassels and sniffing in corners for spiders, until he heard an oil-fired boiler kick into action and sensed the house beginning to warm up. This made him feel a little rest might be in order and so, seeking the safety of his sofa back in the sitting room, he curled up into a neat ball and fell deeply asleep.

As daylight was breaking the human element of the household began to stir. Stuart walked into the sitting room and saw the cat curled up in a ball where they had left him the evening before and he bent down and stroked him lightly on the head.

White Chin opened one eye, purred slightly, and went back to sleep. He heard Anna come downstairs. There was a busy clattering from the kitchen, followed by a squawk of surprise. There were further screeches of outrage as each feline misdemeanour was discovered and Anna's final complaint, loudest of all, came from the shower room, where she stood, surrounded by ripped-up loo roll, staring at the soaking wet lavatory seat.

White Chin's ears flicked as he heard shouts going back and forth between the man and the woman. He sighed deeply and burying his nose under his paw he went back to sleep.

## 7

# For your own good!

As the day went on things got worse. White Chin became nervous. He could sense an atmosphere around the place. He was lying quietly on the sofa, thinking about nothing in particular, when he heard Anna come into the room. She leaned over the sofa and grabbed him roughly by the neck, wearing scratchy rubber gloves.

First she put liquid stuff in his ears and wiped them out with cotton wool. Not nice! Then she held him down and sprayed him all over with some hissing liquid that smelt dreadful. He miaowed and wriggled, trying to get away, but then, worst of all, she wrapped him in a towel so he couldn't move and cut off the tips of his claws. White Chin felt miserable and as soon as Anna released him he ran away and hid under a large brown paper bag in case she came back for more.

As he stared out at her with frightened round eyes, ears pressed back flat in alarm, she bent towards him and whispered, 'You've got to trust me, all that was for your own good! I just had to get rid of your mites and fleas.' She stood up and laughed. 'Not that you'd care, I don't suppose!' Although her voice was gentle, her hands had not been. White Chin dropped his gaze and licked his nose before opening his mouth wide and uttering a long, plaintive miaow.

After this things began slowly to improve. He was given a plate of proper food meant for cats and he ate until he could eat no more. It was good to have a full belly. He also discovered a large bowl of dried cat biscuits, which he liked. The bowl containing them had high sides which bent his stiff white whiskers, so whenever he wanted to eat he filled his mouth with biscuits and then dropped them a few inches away from the bowl. The trouble was that he forgot to eat all the biscuits he had so carefully transported across the floor. He found himself repeatedly fleeing from Anna's agonised cries as she skidded on his abandoned food for the umpteenth time.

Days grew into weeks and in spite of the irritations that the little cat caused to Anna, he continued to enjoy the comfort of the warm house and unlimited food he was given. At no time, however, did he feel completely at ease. There were house rules in place that he didn't properly understand.

Stuart and Anna didn't like him coming upstairs. At night, when they went to bed, they shut their bedroom door. He wanted to sleep in there with them and often waited for the chance to get in and hide, so he would be there before them. But he never remembered in time!

After Stuart and Anna had gone upstairs and the bedroom door was finally closed, White Chin would feel sad. Then he would look around him for something to do. The house had a long wide pine staircase which led to the upper floor and the wood was bare and highly polished. It was the perfect place for a gallop. As he sped up and down the stairs, he would clatter and thump, which was intensely satisfying. There was a little rug that he used as a slide – although he never mastered the skill of getting it back out of the corner where it always ended up! He would do these circuits again and again and he rarely missed a night of such pleasures. Sometimes he could hear muffled voices rising behind the closed door!

Another house rule, which White Chin simply couldn't obey, was to leave the cotton-covered sofa alone. Whenever White Chin got close to it he was possessed by a strong urge to scratch the side or the back of it. He knew the people didn't like it, but he was just beginning to achieve a result. Under the armrest a rather satisfying clump of loosened threads dangled down, inviting his attention each time he walked by.

What was really annoying was that every time he got even close to the sofa either Stuart or, more often, Anna would shout at him. He had learned to wait until he was on his own before sinking in his claws, pulling off their irritating sheaths and scent marking his territory. People didn't seem to understand these things.

A further instance of White Chin's misconduct that taxed the patience of his human companions was that he continued to wee down the hole in the shower room floor whenever he could get in there. The resulting smell was becoming quite overpowering. The door was often kept shut, but White Chin always watched for his chance and was in there, quick as a flash, the second anyone forgot.

The response to this – as to everything White Chin seemed to do – was shouting. The people in this house did lots of that!

As well as enjoying his active life inside the house, White Chin would regularly investigate the territory immediately surrounding his new home, but since the terrible gales he had no wish to return to High Fell Wood. He would hunt down the odd wood mouse, usually because it was there rather than from hunger, but he was warm and well-fed and there seemed little point in going elsewhere. Besides, he enjoyed the company of the man, who, sometimes, when *she* wasn't around, would stroke him.

Kirstie had ridden through the woods on Buster many times since the great gale, but never found any trace of White Chin. She had pestered her long-suffering father to stay on the look out for him on his sheep rounds, but he too had failed to make a sighting. He kept assuring his daughter that White Chin would be fine and would have found a home for the winter, but Kirstie spent many a night tossing and turning, unable to sleep. She would imagine one terrifying episode after another in which her beloved black-and-white cat would find himself on the edge of disaster, and she would descend in the morning with dark shadows under her eyes.

Currently, however, she was filled with thoughts of Christmas and the many school activities associated with it. She wasn't in the Nativity Play as such, but there was the choir, and she had landed the leading role in next term's *Alice the Musical*, which promised to be a major distraction. Also she had just got very involved in making what her teacher called 'fetchings', but which everyone else called fingerless gloves. She had knitted a pair for her mother in bright lilac mohair, a pair for her father in dark brown (suitable for his muddy work she had joked) and a pair for her brother in black on which she had sewn a white skull and crossbones. She was about to start on a pair in scarlet wool with gold flecks for her beloved Gramps. She enjoyed making them, but as they were presents they had to be done in secret, which was time-consuming and took her away from riding Buster and trying to find White Chin.

Tonight the volunteers who had agreed to sing carols were to meet on the green before setting out on the highways and byways of Troonholme village. Kirstie and her brother Alex dutifully wandered up to the green alone to receive their instructions. Their Mum had been delayed and Kirstie knew there was no point in working on her tone-deaf Dad. It was dark and cold by the time everyone was there and Kirstie and Alex giggled as their warm breath shaped itself into dramatic clouds in front of their faces in the torchlight. There were eight carollers in all and Kirstie and Alex were the only children, apart from Baby George – who didn't count because he hadn't volunteered!

It was agreed that the carollers would warm up at Lake House with the American woodcarver, Kay Keble, who lived over the other side of the River Troon, and work their way back over the bridge, past Old Bridge Farm where Kirstie and Alex lived and on around the houses surrounding the green. Finally, if time allowed, they'd go up the hill to the outlying houses near the fell.

The group kept up a spanking pace and never sang more than two carols at any homestead – often only one – the favourite being 'Good King Wenceslas'. Many of the households had 'paid them off', which meant the carollers received money in advance in order for the householder to avoid having singers standing on their doorstep! This habit meant they could get around in double-quick time. Their money box was filling up fast and soon the little band of pilgrims, minus Baby George and his mother, were climbing up the grassy track towards the fell.

As they walked there was much talk about poachers in the area and the discovery of snares in odd places around the woods that had definitely not been placed legally. Doug Wilcock and his wife Bernie were both local gamekeepers and kept a close eye on these matters. Kirstie and Alex listened to this talk in a half-hearted way, but they didn't learn a lot. Kirstie worried about the sound of the snares. It sounded like they would do horrible things to any animals who were caught in them – she heard Doug say the way they were set up was illegal because the animals just choked to death. She found herself shuddering at the thought of it and wondered if she should warn people who had animals that might get caught. At this point all conversation stopped as everyone started panting heavily with the effort of the climb and Kirstie pushed it to the back of her mind.

The last house on the track was Fellside House and Kirstie knew it well as this track was one of several rides that she took with Buster when going up to the fell. She hadn't been this way since the big gale because the route higher up was blocked by a fallen elm tree waiting to be sawn up. Before the singers had even started their first carol, Stuart came to the door waving a ten-pound note, and Doug laughingly enquired if he was trying to pay them off. As they began a brisk version of 'In the Bleak Midwinter' it started to rain, so Stuart invited them all into the hallway and Anna joined them from the sitting room.

Kirstie stopped in her tracks. Through the open door she could see a sofa in front of a large fire. Lying, in splendid state on one end of the sofa, was a small black-and-white cat, who sleepily turned his amber-eyed gaze towards the noise in the hallway.

'White Chin!' Kirstie gasped. She peeled away from the carollers and screwing up her face apologetically at Anna as she pushed past her, she sidled into the sitting room. She flung herself onto her knees in front of the little cat and put her arms around him, murmuring sweet nothings to him and fondling his ears. The cat's eyes widened at the affection he was being shown and his rough pink tongue came out and licked the back of the hand that fussed him. As Kirstie burbled to him, he purred back to her. Anna, who had watched this scene with interest, joined the girl and the cat in the sitting room to find out what was going on.

Kirstie's words fell out in a great rush as she excitedly tried to explain how much she adored the little cat, how she had seen him abandoned and how she had stopped to talk to him whenever she saw him in High Fell Wood. She then went on about how she and Dad couldn't find him on the night of the great storm and since then she'd been worried sick about him and how heavenly it was that here he was, safe and sound all the time.

'Oh Anna, it's so cool he's here. It's just the best early Christmas present in the world to know he's all right and safe with you,' Kirstie chortled happily. Alex, who didn't share his sister's passion for cats, stood in the doorway and groaned when he heard her saying this. Anna laughed and ruffled his hair in sympathy.

She looked across to the little cat lying peacefully on the sofa and, addressing only Alex, said in a very low voice, 'Well, between you and me, that cat there – White Chin as you call him – isn't the most welcome house guest I've ever had and I can't help wondering what Christmas might have in store for us!'

## 8

## Walking in a winter wonderland

As Christmas approached White Chin managed, yet again, to bring disgrace upon himself. It really hadn't been his fault. Well, most of it hadn't been. The day following the carol singing Anna had spent much of the morning decorating a Christmas tree in the hall from top to toe in a silver livery. White Chin had watched her with big eyes as she draped strands of tinsel very precisely over the branches and carefully suspended the heavy mirror-balls in places where they could most easily swivel before finally placing a bright silver star at the very top of the tree.

That afternoon the low winter sun shone through the glass door and struck the countless surfaces of the spinning silver balls, sending a shower of glittering reflections revolving across the floor and walls and up the big curtain by the door. White Chin, enchanted by these sparkling lights, had chased them around the floor, then up the walls. Eventually, when they flickered up the full length of the curtain, he had been unable to contain himself. Before he knew what he was doing he had clawed his way right up to the top trying to catch the shimmering little 'fishes' and then, when he realised they didn't really exist and he needed to get down, he had turned round and got his back leg jammed through one of the large iron curtain rings. When he had miaowed out for help, he had been severely shouted at and then, as Anna lifted him down, yanking out his back leg from where it was held fast, it felt to White Chin as if she shook him so hard that his teeth rattled.

It didn't stop there either. A little later on, when he knew Anna had gone out in the car, he had sprang onto the top of the piano in the hall and from up there he was able to pull off any number of the strings of tinsel adorning the large tree. He held them up on the hook of his long middle claw so they dangled down artfully and then he ate them. One after the other. Like shiny strings of spaghetti. After that he was sick; several times in different rooms as he had to keep moving to ease the pain. There was more shouting.

When they put boxes and squashy things all wrapped up in shiny paper with labels and ribbons under the tree, White Chin had a merry night pulling, chewing and clawing all the ribbons and ripping off the shiny paper. The next day he got shouted at all over again. It was most tiresome. In fact the hubbub was so regular that he started to sleep in the bottom of the airing cupboard from early morning, so that he could pretend the shouting routine was nothing to do with him. This worked until Anna actually found him in the airing cupboard, when he got shouted at straight in his face, loudly, horribly.

As the winter ran its course, the weather changed and got noticeably colder. It had been dry for a long spell but freezing cold days were followed by nights of iron-hard frosts. The wind had been blowing from the east for some days, but then it shifted to the north and rattled at the house with its icy breath. The insides of the windows steamed up as the warmth of indoors met the cold of outside. One evening, when all in the house had gone to their beds, the snow started to fall. It fell silently in large soft flakes all night long. The following morning the eerie blue light creeping around the edge of the curtains, and the strange heavy silence, indicated that the world outside had changed.

White Chin was aware from the subdued sounds outside that something was different, but he couldn't tell what. He had never seen snow. He waited for the household to awake. Stuart was the first one to appear and White Chin heard him laughing as he opened the front door. White Chin trotted across ready to go out.

As the door opened, what greeted him just made him blink, and the brightness hurt his eyes. He smelt the air. All the scents that should have been there were muted. Sounds that he would normally expect to hear in this familiar territory of his were silenced. And where was everything? What had happened? All the bushes and plants had disappeared and they had been replaced by crouching humps with white whiskers. He could see the bench where he had sat only three days before when the sun was shining, but it had grown into a queer fluffy shape. There was no green grass to be seen anywhere. Everything in the world had changed to black and white. White Chin was mystified. He hesitated on the doorstep but suddenly he felt a gentle push from the man behind him and the door was clicked shut. He was out in it, whatever it was!

White Chin couldn't believe the cold of this white stuff. It was extraordinary. It was wet like water, but somehow solid. He put just one foot in at first – terrible! He pulled it out, then he did that with each foot in turn. It didn't get any better. As he shook each paw energetically he nearly fell over. As he moved forward, holding his tail clear of the snow, he arched his back to try to keep his tummy from scraping the cold wetness. He waddled unsteadily with his feet wide apart. He heard the man laugh and, as he turned, he saw him disappear inside the house.

Quickly, however the little cat realised that underneath the snow everything smelt as it had before and that it was all the same really, it just looked different. On seeing something large poking up through the snow, he put out his right paw nervously to touch it. It was only a twig and it had been there yesterday. He started to play with it. A crow flapped slowly overhead, croaking an investigative 'craaar, craaaar'. Soon White Chin was exploring every corner of this new snowy world with delight and his joy knew no bounds when he discovered a transparent lid of ice covering the garden pond. This was, luckily for him, thick enough to take his weight. As he walked across this newly solid water the bright goldfish beneath the ice started to dart around quickly when they saw him looming above them. So he ran across the slippery surface to try to catch them.

The run became an astonishing slide with his legs spreading ever wider as he went. To save himself he jumped in the air, turning in the opposite direction. The fish beneath doubled back to get away so White Chin stopped and spun round after them. The fish then swam randomly all about the pond. At this point White Chin stopped running and with great effort he tried to pounce forcefully through the solid water, skidding again as he met the resisting ice. The fish fled and hid themselves beneath their weed. White Chin looked up at the sky and yawned.

The cold spell ended as abruptly as it had started and soon the world was drippily returning to the way that White Chin expected it to be. Kirstie had called to see him once since Christmas, and now the thaw had started, she called again. They spent a cosy ten minutes sitting on the garden bench talking to each other. At least she talked to White Chin whilst she stroked him and he purred back. She was the only human in his world whom he really trusted and he was always sad to see her leave. He tried to let her see that was how he felt, but he never knew if she understood.

There were many signs of spring in the air and the small mammals that White Chin loved to hunt were beginning to make their presence felt. The native birds too were already rehearsing their dawn choruses, kicked off by the early robin who was soon joined by the blackbirds and thrushes. White Chin started to spend more of his day outside actively hunting.

He was having trouble with a tiresome year-old magpie, who kept taunting him. White Chin would be sitting in the garden, minding his own business, or more likely that of a tasty wood mouse, when this bumptious black-and-white bounder would flap about behind him, chattering noisily, jumping up and down and bouncing up really close. One particular morning the young magpie was joined by another. Together they 'worked' the cat as a team until he became annoyed and increasingly alarmed. They simply wouldn't leave him alone. The final outrage was when he was concentrating on one of them, and the other crept in behind him and tweaked his tail – hard.

White Chin spun into action. He revolved round in the air and pounced on the culprit. He winded the bird with his forefeet and clamped it firmly in his jaws feeling both angry and triumphant. Instead of giving the bird the killing bite, as he usually would, he carried him alive into the house as a present for his humans. The cat proudly placed the bird on the ground in front of them both, but the maimed magpie started to flutter and White Chin had to pounce on him and rip out mouthfuls of feathers to show who was boss. What happened next dumbfounded White Chin. He had expected praise and instead he was deafened by terrified screams from Anna. Stuart wasn't much better as, shouting loudly, he frantically hit out with a broom, smashing the bird to the ground with it. Before White Chin knew what had happened, Stuart had picked him up by the scruff of his neck and thrown him into the garden, mumbling things that the little cat didn't understand.

White Chin picked himself up and started to groom himself. From time to time, mid-lick, he would pause, leg pointing skywards, puzzled. After he had tidied himself up he walked towards the potting shed, feeling hurt. After more kerfuffle inside the house the front door was opened and the dead magpie was also thrown out. Shortly afterwards the door opened again and a blizzard of white, black and shimmering blue and purple feathers snowed gently onto the ground to join the corpse from which they had been ripped. White Chin watched from a distance. Dead magpies were not very interesting.

That night White Chin waited outside the front door to be let in but, in spite of his repeated miaowings, for the first time the door remained closed to him.

In the morning, had the residents of Fellside House heart enough to care, they would have seen one small black-and-white cat squashed into the top of an old flowerpot urn, watching the house, with a strange expression on his face.

## 9

## By his wild lone

Inside the house the humans had a long discussion about what to do about 'that darned cat.' Their voices rose and fell and then, at length, a silence reigned. Anna had always had mixed feeling about the little cat in their midst, from the first night he had entered their house. She knew that Stuart had a soft spot for him, but she personally found him tiresome, noisy and difficult, and really didn't see the point of him.

Stuart in his heart had known that the ongoing battle to give the cat a home was lost from the moment White Chin had started to use their shower as his toilet and the magpie episode was simply the final straw. The point of no return had finally been reached. The cat could stay in the garden, but he was no longer allowed inside their house.

White Chin was bewildered. The potting shed window remained open and a bowl of dried cat food was left on the floor, so it seemed he was allowed to go in there. But at last it became clear to him that he wasn't to go back into the house. He had tried several times and it was always the same. He got shouted at by both of them. Sometimes he would see Stuart and Anna, together and separately, but the door was never opened to him again and they rarely spoke to him – not that he gave them much opportunity.

High Fell Wood became ever more appealing and White Chin started to hunt deeper and more earnestly than he had ever done before. He spent long moments sitting on his favourite hill looking down the valley, working things out in his head. This was the territory that he knew best and the world of people had let him down, yet again. In the first few days after he had been banned from the house, he had eaten the food that Stuart and Anna left in the shed for him, but he had spent little time around the house and garden. Bit by bit he became again a creature of the wet wild woods and soon he abandoned the shed altogether and moved back into a cave up in High Fell Wood. This world, filled with wondrous numbers of animals and birds, with its amazing smells, and its astonishing sounds meant freedom. White Chin felt he could be himself. A cat who could walk wherever he wanted, whenever he wanted. Yes, it meant he would forfeit the security of the shed and the easy food, but it also meant there would be no people shouting at him morning, noon or night. People were not to be trusted. He would be his own cat.

Things in the wood were beginning to change. It was now mid-February and although the weather remained unsettled, on warm days many of the dormant animals were venturing forth to get a quick meal before returning to finish their winter slumbers. The hunting was becoming easier. Through the day, as the birds sang to claim their breeding territories, the woods vibrated with sound. The animals of the night also made their presence known. There had been a vicious-sounding fight between two dog foxes over the carcass of a pheasant, which had attracted a vixen looking to scavenge any pickings. Her presence at the scene extended the length of the brawl, and the sound of it carried over many acres. For several nights following this White Chin was woken not only by foxes barking but also loud screaming. It was the spine-chilling sound of a vixen calling for a dog fox and no male fox for miles around would have been in any doubt of the message. The call made the little tomcat strangely uneasy.

White Chin was changing. Having got back into some of his old routines he soon became restless and yearned to explore new pastures. Something powerful was stirring within him, making him want to move on.

He found himself prowling the fell and repeatedly scenting the air. The time was right to leave and he felt an urge to head for the distant river in the valley bottom. His only problem was working out his route. From the garden of Fellside House he had often listened to the big tractors and giant log wagons trundling along the village road below the fell. He had no wish to meet them.

His hunting trips had taught him that he could journey to the bottom of the fell along the woodland paths avoiding the road completely and this would eventually lead him to open fields bordered by dry stone walls. Beyond that it was unknown territory. White Chin set off and in no time at all he had managed to skirt round the edge of the village, only crossing the main road once. He followed several different sheep tracks, but, finding himself drawn in one direction, he changed tack and instead allowed his nose to lead him through field after field. He only moved off course to use gates and other openings which were easy to climb through and he covered a good distance in a short time. The birds sounded different here. Their calls lacked the intensity of the woodland songs. And the smells were also different. White Chin was entering a new world. He paused for a small snack of field vole and drank some brackish water from a rusty upturned tin can.

As he resumed his journey, the field White Chin now found himself crossing was bordered on one side by a small road which passed down the side of a farm. As he drew close to the farm he listened for sounds of life. A dog whined in a bored, chained-up sort of way and a man whistled as he hammered at some loose panelling on a farm outbuilding. White Chin paused thoughtfully as he scented the man. He knew that smell! He sniffed around the gate and then he found he recognised another scent. Kirstie! He could tell that she had passed between these gateposts many times. Was she in there? He was curious.

There was a post holding a swinging wrought iron sign declaring this place to be Old Bridge Farm. A large cattle grid lay between the gateposts that White Chin couldn't cross, so he squeezed under the gate and turned down the wide driveway. It was pitted with holes and puddles, and was rich with smells. He detected two cats, both strangers to him. One male, the other female. He could smell and, he now realised, hear, Shep, whose scent he knew. And another scent he recognised was Buster, the pony. There were numerous other animal smells across the driveway and around the yard, but none of them were familiar in any way. He smelt people he didn't know, as well as Kirstie's Dad, John, who was the one whistling, and everywhere he could smell Kirstie. He walked up the path to the front door and turned round and sprayed the stone doorposts. Having left the information that he had called, he squeezed back under the gate and walked on down the road.

White Chin didn't know why, but the river seemed always to lure him on. He felt he was being tugged towards it. He left the road and headed for the sound of rushing water. As he got closer to his goal he could hear the tinkling of thousands of droplets as they tumbled over the stony riverbed. The cat ran up a small mound and there before him at last, wide and shining, lay the River Troon, glinting in the sun. He climbed down to the water's edge. It was deliciously clear. Stirring the water with his paw, he drank deep. Then he sniffed the air; something thrilled him. White Chin stood still and gazed ahead, dreamily. He walked along the bank side and scented the ground with great concentration. He could smell one of his own kind. His hair stood on end with pleasure. It was a special smell. It excited him in a way that the other cat smells hadn't. It was the scent of a young female cat in her prime.

White Chin looked upriver to see that the small road he had walked on from the farm continued over an old arched bridge and beyond. He walked along the bank and jumped over a wall onto the road. As he turned to cross the bridge he picked up new feline scents. One of them was the female. The other was male and a stranger – although not from the farm. He trotted across the bridge and then stopped.

There before him, to one side of the road, lay a large lake fed by water running through a weir from the river. Beyond the lake stood a low sandstone building reflected in the water. The cat was looking at Lake House, an old cornmill that had stood on the River Troon for over 400 years, and was now occupied by the woodcarver, Kay Keble. Tall trees towered behind the house, signalling the beginnings of Troonholme Park. White Chin had, without knowing it, entered a large country estate.

He looked across the lake and saw the shadowlike figure of a grey cat move back into the trees. When he scented the air, he realised that this was the male cat whose footsteps he had marked on the bridge.

White Chin walked around the edge of the lake towards the house. As he approached, he found a sheltered paved area near the main door. And there, lying in regal splendour, was a handsome long-haired cat. She was of the breed of Maine Coone, but all that White Chin knew was that she was beautiful. She lifted her head and as he drew nearer she silently thrashed her magnificent plumed tail. White Chin had never seen a cat like her in his life. He stopped and stared, his nose twitching as never before.

As the tail of the goddess in front of him thrashed more violently, he delicately backed away a few yards and sat down. He was enchanted by the presence of this astonishing creature. When he had first picked up the scent of this cat he had become slightly excited. But now, as he watched her, nothing else in the world mattered any more. Only her. She was perfection. Her coat was white and lush, enhanced by tiny splashes of red and brown on her back and near her ear. Her great tail was a perfect feathery brush of light red. It was a tail that most cats can only dream of! Above her right eye she had a dark line like a singular black eyebrow, and she had a superb ruff of fine white fur and long tufts around her ears. She was regal!

The white queen stared back at the tomcat facing her, with unblinking green eyes. Suddenly she opened her mouth wide and yawned dismissively. She rose, stretched casually, and without a backward glance at her new admirer, slid gracefully through a cat flap in the door, disappearing from his sight. White Chin stared at the place where she had stood, stunned.

The day before White Chin started out on his great expedition Kirstie launched herself into travels of her own. She decided to spend part of a weekend with her Gramps for a long overdue visit. Gramps, her mother's father, was a retired doctor who lived on his own in a great big rambling house across the far side of the county. Only rarely could Gramps be persuaded to come out of it. Kirstie's mother, Joan, had taken over all manner of goodies for him just before Christmas, together with his presents, so that he would have a properly festive time on his own, knowing that he would refuse to up sticks and visit them.

Joan had driven Kirstie across and was to collect her again on Sunday afternoon. As Kirstie arrived she was met by a hugely enthusiastic Gramps who was waving his red fingerless gloves at her, beaming his head off. He was far more pleased with them than anyone else in her family had been with theirs. Kirstie grinned to herself, wondering if he ever actually took them off! He insisted on calling them his 'fetching fetchings' and kept waving them with great pride at her, or anyone else who came to the house. It was embarrassing, really.

Kirstie and her Gramps were very close and shared a lot of interests. One of the things they both equally loved was Gramps reading books aloud to her at bedtime. Kirstie knew she was really too old for it and would never tell her schoolfriends, but she loved it, especially because they had really good talks about all sorts of things as well as the story. The current book on the go was *Tarka the Otter*. Gramps was a brilliant reader and did lots of different voices. And he was a terrible tease, leaving Kirstie at a cliffhanger, hardly able to sleep, wondering what was going to happen next, even when she knew really!

In return Kirstie tried to help the old man with his numerous tasks in the garden. It was big. He was always throwing himself into jobs with enormous zeal and then falling over and banging or cutting himself. Kirstie could hardly remember a time when he didn't have elastoplasts stuck on his hands or his head. At the moment he had one on his right thumb, and Kirstie wondered whether it would have been better to knit him proper gloves with fingers instead.

While Kirstie was with Gramps she started to tell him about White Chin. Gramps was himself an animal lover and Kirstie knew if she could only explain it properly he would understand why White Chin had become so special to her. She really wanted him to understand. Gramps had had dogs and cats around him as long as Kirstie could remember. But his much-loved yellow lab had died just before Gran, three years ago and he was adamant he wouldn't have another animal. Once when Kirstie had asked him why he had replied:

'Well, Kirstie, Thomas Edison said it better than I can. He said, "I'm long on ideas, but short on time. I expect to live to be only about a hundred."' And with that Gramps had laughed, content enough to be on his own, it seemed, until he reached a hundred.

Now Kirstie tried harder than ever to explain the way that White Chin had captured her heart. She described his funny white markings and his wonky white chin; his long lanky legs and black silky fur. She talked of how, on the rare occasions he had sat on her knee or licked her hair or hand, her heart had fluttered from the pure pleasure of his closeness. She talked of his deep, wonderful, loving purr. She looked up at Gramps with an intensity that made the old man's face crease into deep smiles, as she described the power of White Chin's eyes. Their magical golden amber depths and the way that when he looked at her, really looked at her, she felt as if he was looking into her soul.

'I'm not imagining it. The way he stares I mean. It's kind of serious and deep but sort of into you. His eyes are huge and very wide apart and when he looks at you he somehow looks at more than just your face. He stares into somewhere deep inside you!'

Gramps, trying not to laugh, covered his mouth with the back of his hand.

'Ah – like an X-ray machine, you mean?' he said mock gravely.

Kirstie waved her hand impatiently, sad that he wasn't taking her seriously.

'No, please listen to me. It's like he's got these deep feelings that he's trying to communicate. More than any cat I've ever met, it feels like he wants to love and be loved, it feels like . . .' her voice faltered. She walked across the room and gazed, unseeing, through the window. In her mind's eye she could see White Chin's intense, triangular little face, his majestic whiskers and those wonderful golden eyes.

She said in a tiny voice, 'It – he – feels really special, that's all. It's hard to explain.' While she had been staring out of the window Gramps had been watching her closely. He now waved a scarlet mitt at her to catch her eye and grinned at her kindly.

'I know, Kirstie. I do. These things are hard to put into words. But some animals have that effect on a chap, I know that. A bond is created between the two of you and you respond to that particular animal more strongly than to any other. That animal takes ownership of you in some way and it sounds to me as if this White Chin has done this to you.' He walked across to her and placing his hand gently on her back he bent down to look questioningly up at her face. His granddaughter grinned at him lopsidedly and nodded.

'Kirstie, I look forward to meeting him the next time I come over. I am sure he is all that you say he is and I am sure I will enjoy becoming the latest victim of his penetrating gaze.'

'Oh I do hope so, but I must warn you, he can be ever so hard to track down. I could never find him in the woods if he didn't want me to. Still at least I know where he is at the moment!' Kirstie smiled happily.

On returning home from Gramps, with her thoughts now firmly on White Chin, Kirstie decided to go up to Fellside House and see that all was well with the little cat. She grabbed her bike and clattered off. Anna was out when she arrived, and Stuart seemed embarrassed when he understood the purpose of Kirstie's call. He shrugged and at first all he said was that White Chin had 'gone walkies'.

Kirstie had to fight really hard to hold back the tears. It was some time before she managed to piece things together, and only after Stuart had explained that Anna had simply been unable to cope with the cat's various misdeeds did Kirstie fully understand that White Chin had been banned from the house. Stuart, perhaps out of some feeling of guilt, took Kirstie out to the potting shed and showed her the untouched bowl of cat food.

Kirstie, now in despair, left her bike against their garden wall and clambered up the track into High Fell Wood. As she walked she tried to imagine what being thrown out of the house by Anna and Stuart would do to White Chin's trust of people. First he'd been dumped in the woods by those horrible men and now this. It was too awful.

She kept calling his name repeatedly. Finally, as darkness started to fall, she knew she should return home.

When she got back to her shiny new bike, for no good reason other than that it was there she kicked it, angrily, right in the middle of its frame. The pedal whacked back on her foot and made her hop about from the pain of it. She mounted it crossly, foot throbbing, and headed for home. As she bumped her way down the steep hills and country lanes towards Old Bridge Farm all her pent-up frustrations welled out of her in tears, unchecked, and she sobbed aloud. She had lost him again!

# 10

## For everything there is a season

White Chin felt awed by the imposing house, whose shadow now fell across him as the sun dropped low. Or was it something else that was causing his heart to hammer? He sauntered along the lakeside, scenting the air and the ground intensely. Slowly the little cat made a thorough investigation of the garden, circling the house several times. Using every sense available to him he was soaking up any smell, sound, sight, taste and touch that might tell him more about that magnificent female cat he had just met.

By that one act of crossing the bridge and turning through the gates he had entered into a different world and his old world had ceased to exist. His mind was

tormented by the thought of the bewitching long-haired cat who had vanished through the mysterious hole in the door. Who was she? Where had she gone? When would he see her again? Her smell was everywhere and small strands of her fur, which had snagged on branches as she had walked by, brushed teasingly against him as he passed.

Dusk deepened into dark. The cat sat down by the wall. He was perfectly still, but for the tip of his tail which twitched, repeatedly, as if it had a mind of its own. As White Chin stared out into the velvety shadows around him he felt a turmoil of emotions. He was unsure what to do and he was frightened.

Eventually White Chin rose and stretched lengthily, knowing one thing for sure: it was plain hunger that was nagging at his belly. The owls had been calling for some minutes and were in full voice as he walked out of the garden and made for the tree-clad acres beyond.

The lie of Troonholme Park was very different from High Fell Wood. There were wide avenues running through these woods that would take a vehicle, the trees ran along the valley bottom and there were traces of many rabbits. The cat encountered one almost immediately. But the rabbit, on sighting him, thumped the ground hard in warning to others, before flashing his white tail and racing into the shelter of the undergrowth to disappear from sight. White Chin didn't attempt any pursuit.

The hunting was good however, as having started

with a wood mouse, he then caught his first fully-grown pheasant. She had been roosting too close to the ground and he was surprised at how clumsy her attempt to fly away had been. He got her around the back of her neck and killed her quickly, but she squawked a great deal and flapped her wings. The feathers proved a problem to begin with, but once he had mouthed them away from the body, he found the meat was good. So large was the pheasant that he couldn't finish it and had to dig the remains into a shallow grave for future use, leaving a spill of feathers on the ground. Having eaten his fill, White Chin continued on his quest.

At the far side of the woods, the trees gave way to rushes and heather and the land climbed upwards, ever higher into a vast moorland. It stretched way beyond the little cat's vision. White Chin was tense with curiosity. He held his body still but his eyes moved rapidly, scanning a wide area, and his ears revolved 180 degrees, absorbing every sound like a radar dish. Lifting his head high, his nostrils twitched as he unriddled the wind.

Kirstie rushed out of the farmhouse, banging the door behind her. She grabbed her bike, switched on the lights and started to cycle down the road towards the bridge.

It had been wonderful seeing Gramps, but from the moment she had got up to Fellside House and discovered

the dreadful news about White Chin, everything had started to go wrong. It had gone from bad to worse when, on reaching home, she had tried to explain why the little cat meant so much to her and why she passionately needed to find him and give him a home. Her Mum and Dad hadn't reacted as she had expected. Instead, while she had eaten her tea, she had been given a boring lecture about how she didn't spend enough time at home looking after the animals as it was. And then her Mum had gone on about Buster being neglected, and how he was just left standing unridden in the field or the stable. Kirstie had hotly denied that she didn't spend enough time with Buster, but she had got nowhere and she had run out. She needed to get away from this nagging. Somewhere, anywhere.

As Kirstie rattled towards the bridge her mind was full of thoughts of how her Mum really didn't understand how many things she had to grapple with in her life. She realised that without thinking about it she had started to head for Kay Keble's house. Kay would understand exactly what she was on about; she loved animals and anyway she was fun to be with, unlike some!

Her thoughts were rudely interrupted by an approaching battered grey car, which whooshed over the bridge straight at her, blinding her with its lights as it sped towards Troonholme village. She slammed on her brakes and fell into the hedge, gasping first in surprise and then in pain. Although the windows of the car had been steamed up, she thought she had seen two figures inside – the driver looked vaguely familiar, but she was too shaken to pay much attention. If she hadn't swerved into the hedge they would have hit her. She collected herself and continued on her way to Lake House. She propped her bike against the lakeside wall and rang the bell of the studio next to the house, brushing herself down from her fall.

The door of the studio, once the barn to the corn mill, opened wide to reveal a willowy young woman with wispy long blonde hair, clad in a full-length black apron and waving a pointed wood rasp. When she saw that Kirstie was her visitor, one of her finely manicured eyebrows shot up questioningly, and then her bright red lips parted in a broad smile of welcome

'Hi, honey! How lovely to see you! Come in, come in. Come and have a cup of something. What would you like?'

This felt a load better than that scene back in the kitchen at home. Kirstie returned her grin gratefully.

'Oh Kay, are you sure? I'm sorry to just turn up but it's so HORRIBLE at home! It's all been AWFUL.' And she flopped down gratefully onto the studio couch, making herself comfortable. Kay bustled off to the little annexe and put the kettle on.

As she waited for the kettle to boil Kirstie got up again and started to peer happily about her. She loved coming into the studio. Everything in this room was somehow magical. Kay was a woodcarver who did tiny boxwood carvings of animals like harvest mice and wrens and toads and cockerels and bats and prawns. They were exquisite and each one took her many weeks of work. She called them netsukes. The most complicated ones could take her up to a year to complete. Looking around at the animals on her trays was like coming into an Aladdin's cave or an Ark for singletons!

Kay re-entered the room bearing steaming mugs and gave a deep, throaty gurgle of pleasure as she took in the absorbed interest on Kirstie's face. Kirstie was holding up Kay's current work-in-progress. It consisted of a tiny harvest mouse who was slowly being chipped and chiselled out of the hard ball of boxwood to emerge from a beautiful conical shell. When Kirstie handed it back reverently to its sculptor she told Kay she reckoned she was sure she'd seen its tiny eye wink at her.

Kirstie snuggled down, mug in hand, and they chatted about all manner of things. Eventually, however, Kay, realising that something was afoot, managed to get the young girl to unload her woes.

Kirstie loved talking to this sophisticated young woman. She was feisty and in some ways like a much older sister – although she was outspoken, she was a good listener too. Kay nodded in exactly the right understanding kind of way when Kirstie tried to explain about White Chin; why she felt the way she did and why she was desperate to give him a home.

After Kirstie had reached the end of the White Chin saga, Kay started to tell her what had been happening in her neck of the woods. 'Involving,' she said sarcastically, 'my jolly old neighbours the other side of the wood.'

'What, Doug, the gamekeeper?' Kirstie asked, nervously. This handsome woman with the bright eyes and rasping trans-Atlantic voice was a sculptor of renown, and she had a reputation for being headstrong. The artist looked down at the small carving in front of her through narrowed eyes and nodded. Kirstie saw the muscles in Kay's jaw flex, like they did when she was cross.

'Yup. The very same. He's an awkward so-and-so. All I did was to ask him, quite politely, to remove his vile Larsen traps.' Kay stood up and poured more coffee. Kirstie kept quiet to see what was coming next. Kay went on, 'Trouble is . . . it upsets me seeing those wretched magpies, jumping up and down and screeching out. I can't bear cruelty to animals. The cage is on his land, the other side of the lake, but it's in full view of me and anyone who comes to see me here.' Kay stopped.

Kirstie waited a little before saying, 'I don't like those traps either, but Dad says magpies are a bad lot. They kill loads of wild birds, not just pheasant chicks, and they take eggs and things – they need to be controlled.' As Kirstie said this she could see that she was making no impact on Kay. In fact as a farmer's daughter she knew that there was a very good reason for keeping down the number of magpies. They had a bad effect on native wild birds as well as pheasants. What Kirstie never understood was why the trapped bird didn't warn other birds away, instead of attracting them in. As soon as one magpie had been caught, it would be caged in the Larsen trap with food and water. Because it bounced about, sometimes as many as two or three further magpies would think the original one had some wonderful treat in there and they would walk straight through the trapdoor to join it.

'Well, anyway, he completely ignored my request.' Kay continued. And then chortling she added, 'So I waited till he'd cleared off and then I popped across and opened the cage door and let it free.'

Kirstie sat back, shocked.

'Ooooh no, Kay. He'll go mad. It takes them ages to catch a magpie in the first place!'

'Well, he won't ever be able to prove it was me, will he? I will say it was the wind that did it, or maybe one of my friends or something.'

She leaned forward. 'Now do me a favour, young lady, will you? Don't you go telling your Dad what I've just told you. You and I have an understanding about animals, but not everyone thinks like we do.'

They both fell silent as Kay gouged tiny pieces of wood from the carving in front of her, revealing more of the true shape of the mouse that it would finally become.

Kirstie knew well from both her parents that there was little love lost between the resident gamekeepers, Doug and his wife Bernie, and their fiery neighbour

Kay. The gamekeepers had the difficult task of running Troonholme Park Manor which was one of the largest shooting estates in the area. The group of businesses that leased the property expected their visiting clients to leave with a full bag of game, regardless of their shooting skills. It was a tall order for two just gamekeepers.

Having been born and raised on a farm, Kirstie knew that surviving on the land either as a farmer or a gamekeeper was hard enough. Disputes between neighbours were to be avoided whenever possible, as they could do untold and lasting damage. She most certainly didn't want to be pulled into a row between Kay and the gamekeepers, who in the end were country people as she herself was.

But as the young girl glanced up at Kay fiercely concentrating on her carving, she realised that she found this woman's approach to life exciting and different. She was fun to be with. Kay laughed a lot. She would dance at the drop of a hat and she would think nothing of throwing off all her clothes and swimming in the lake. All that would ever stop her was the temperature of the water. Kay Keble was a woman of enthusiasms. And, very importantly to Kirstie, she was passionate about animals. *All* animals, and you could see this in her beautiful carvings. She understood why they mattered as much or even more than people mattered. Most adults didn't.

Kay groaned loudly and stood up, stretching her

back. She carefully laid down her gouger and her rasp.

'Right, that's it! That will have to do for the day. My eyes are getting tired. OK, young woman. Tell me more about this little cat of yours.'

Kirstie needed no encouragement and started right in about his black colouring and his funny white chin and white bib and paws and how utterly adorable he was.

'With that colouring, honey, what you have there is a perfect tuxedo cat. You know, like the outfit a man wears to a smart event. He sounds like a grand boy,' Kay said.

'Oh is *that* why you call them tuxedo cats? Gosh, I never understood it before. I would call him a jellicle cat like in the poem. You know, jellicle cats are black and white, jellicle cats go out at night.' She spun around madly, and with a spectacular flourish, waved her imaginary black-and-white tail. But as she flopped down laughing, she remembered and her grin faded.

'Oh, Kay, it's so difficult. I'd love it if White Chin was mine, but ... but ...' and she pulled a tragically sad face.

Kay put her arm around Kirstie's shoulders and gave her a hug. She told her that it wasn't as bad as all that and the answer was to plan ahead. If she could work out when she had to do her schoolwork and when she had proper spare time for riding Buster, she could allocate her time accordingly. And if her mother thought she was really trying with Buster, for example, Kirstie would find that the pressure at home would come off.

'You think?' It sounded hard but Kirstie thought she could give it a go. As Kirstie got up to leave she asked Kay about her own beautiful cat, Adorabelle.

'Ah la belle Adorabelle, she's fine. Indeed, I'd be prepared to bet that at this very moment she's probably lying flat out on my bed upstairs, amusing herself from time to time by poking her outrageous talons into my precious silk quilt. She likes her creature comforts, that little madam, and she has a mind of her own. I worry on and off about when I should take her to the vet to stop her having kittens as she's now old enough. But soon . . . soon!' Kay turned away and took a thoughtful swig out of her mug of coffee, pulling a face as she realised it was cold.

Kirstie stood up to go. As she clambered into her jacket she said, 'I keep worrying about where White Chin has got to. I do hope he's OK?'

'I'm sure he will be, honey. Cats find people, more often than people find cats!' Kay looked across at the young girl's forlorn face and gave her a warm smile, shaking her finger kindly. The message was clear: don't worry.

Kirstie felt, as she almost always did after seeing Kay, that maybe it would be all right after all. They said their farewells to each other and Kirstie let herself out.

As she started to put on her helmet she looked up at the sky. It was dark, and thick fluffy clouds scudded past quickly. A small breeze rustled the leaves, but otherwise there wasn't a sound.

She flipped on her lights and started to pedal through the gates and down the hill. Two chewed-up pheasant feathers blew, unnoticed, across the road and caught in the hedge.

# 11

## A time to embrace

White Chin had spent a considerable time up on the edge of the moorland, determining whether there were any other cats in the neighbourhood. But the great empty spaces and the winds that blew across them unsettled him. He knew, instinctively, that he would feel safer back in the shelter of the woodland behind him. Woods he understood. As he doubled back on his tracks he realised that he wanted more than anything to be in the presence of the beautiful long-haired cat he had seen that afternoon. And some instinct made him want to sort out that mysterious grey cat.

He returned through the woods slowly, remembering the scents and sounds of landmarks for future use.

Along the main track he suddenly smelt a familiar scent. A man-smell from a long time ago. It made his hackles rise. Memories of struggling in that horrible sack they had stuffed him in flashed across his mind. He paused and scented the air for a long time. Reassured that the man was no longer around, White Chin walked on, waving his tail.

He reached Lake House, home of the she-cat whom he wanted to see. As he padded around the outside of the house he became aware of another human scent. A familiar one, that gave him pleasure. He could smell Kirstie! She had been there recently, but now she too had gone.

White Chin went towards the door where he had last seen Adorabelle. Putting his head down he let his lower jaw drop so his mouth hung open. He was sucking up her scent into the roof of his mouth. The smell told him she had not emerged from the house since last he was here. But the grey cat had been here more recently than Adorabelle. More recently, even, than White Chin.

White Chin started. He had an announcement to make. He rolled on the path and rubbed his back and ears over the paving stones. He scent marked, sprayed or rubbed himself against every post and paving stone and jutting object that Adorabelle and any other cat might go anywhere near. He was telling the world that he, White Chin, was here. He became totally absorbed in what he was doing, like an animal possessed. Things had changed. Something had happened that meant he would never be the same again. The feeling of need and longing within him was so intense that it actually made him ache. He yearned for his own kind.

At last the time came when White Chin felt he should find shelter. Earlier in the day when he had done his long investigation he had found a stone shed with a broken door on the far side of the studio. He had seen a big pile of dust sheets in one corner that would make a warm bed.

White Chin slept for some of the night in his shed, but his mind was too full of thoughts of the beautiful cat who was lying somewhere close by for him to sleep long. There was nothing for it, he had to call her out. He sat himself down outside the door, where she had disappeared – he had never before seen a cat flap, so had no idea what it was or how it worked. It looked to him like a closed door.

He heard himself, to his own surprise, making a strange low beseeching call. It was both loving and demanding at the same time. It chirred out of him without his having any control over it. In some ways it was like the call a mother cat makes to her kittens when she wants them to feed from her, only deeper and more masculine. As he paused between calls, the cat flap clacked open and he fell silent. He was now in the presence of the amazing Adorabelle, who stood before him waving her magnificent plumed tail. She looked at him through wide eyes, her expression friendly, but then she walked away and sat down with her back to him.

White Chin was uncertain what to do. He slowly followed her, but circled widely so that he ended up in front of her. Instinct told him to make sure she could see him, as well as hear and smell him. The young tom stood a few feet from her but kept his distance. Adorabelle glanced at him and looked away, but she didn't move.

The two cats stayed like this for some time. The moonlight came and went behind moving banks of cloud, but the pair paid no heed to it. Their awareness of each other was as sharp as if they had been in full sun until the power of the moment was disturbed by a small sound near the gates. White Chin was facing that way and saw the flicker of a dark blue shadow, but more distinctly he smelt it. That grey cat had arrived. When White Chin looked across at Adorabelle, her ears were rotating and he saw her delicate pink nose twitch. She knew the cat was there. White Chin tensed. The grey cat approached. He was lean and sinewy, taller than White Chin and longer in the body. He moved with stealthy grace. As he came nearer he gave a low challenging growl.

White Chin, although the smaller cat, was well-muscled and his wild living had taught him speed and courage. White Chin braced himself for action but at that moment Adorabelle stood up as if neither of the male cats were there, turned tail and walked through the cat flap showing them both a clean pair of heels. Immediately the grey-haired cat, Blue, melted back into the shadows leaving the forlorn White Chin alone in the darkness.

White Chin called to Adorabelle on two more occasions through the night, but she paid no attention to him and at his second attempt, as he was building up to a peak of passion, a light went on upstairs and a window was flung open. Kay Keble's tousled head leaned out and her angry-looking mouth shouted sharp things at him. When he didn't immediately stop calling, she went away only to return with a jug of cold water, which she flung over him. White Chin stopped then and blinked in surprise. With head hung low he shook himself and went away to the shed, where he finally dozed fitfully.

This edgy courtship continued on and off for a further two days and nights. White Chin knew by instinct, from the scent that Adorabelle was leaving all over the place, that she was going to come in heat shortly and would be wanting to mate. Adorabelle, however, who was young and inexperienced, was confused by her emotions and all the attention and inclined to be haughty.

On the third night of his pursuit, White Chin lifted his head to call to Adorabelle with his low soothing chirr, and as his deep purring call echoed out, at last she answered him with her own song, a high-pitched, feminine call making his heart bound with joy. Together they moved off towards the woods and serenaded each other, losing all sense of time or place. White Chin wanted only to walk by her side, until the instant when she would be ready for him.

That was when Blue appeared. He had been waiting for his chance and had snaked through the trees as fluid as water. As White Chin sensed the presence of his rival, he was gripped by a greater anger and ferocity than he had ever felt in his life. His muscles contracted. Every hair on his body became erect. He seemed to swell in size by half again and around his neck his ruff rose like a giant collar.

He advanced towards Blue on stiff legs, sideways, placing each spread paw on the ground with exaggerated gentleness, claws unsheathed and lethal. All the while he howled in a strident, penetrating scream. This was no plaintive mewling for love. This was a full-throated war cry.

Blue, who had expected minor resistance from the younger cat, was not prepared for this. To begin with he snarled his defence, but as the howl rose and White Chin's appearance changed, he stiffened with fear. White Chin, blind to the danger of the fight, started to close in. Blue licked his nose then started to run. White Chin started after him but then collected himself.

Adorabelle had watched all this in silence. She now bowed to White Chin in praise of his valour. She sidled towards him, her head down, glancing at him sideways. She danced for him; she rolled for him; she played with him; she mewed to him. She licked him; she rubbed him; she purred to him. Through the night again and again they chased and caught each other, let each other go and started over again until at last, they mated.

Shortly before dawn Adorabelle, whose beautiful silky white fur was now dirty, wet and bedraggled from all their tussling, retired through her cat flap into the depths of the house to rest and to recover herself. White Chin, having drunk at the shore of the lake, returned to the shed. It was sheltered and quiet and he sat on guard for a while outside the door, looking about him. He squeezed himself through the hole in the door, collapsed on his back on a huge pile of dustsheets and sank into the deepest sleep of his life.

## 12

## A time to seek

White Chin awoke at first light aching from hunger. With joy in his heart and feeling heroic he walked out into the morning. He was going hunting and he would return with a trophy for his love.

He went first to the hidey-hole where he had attempted to bury the pheasant he had killed three days earlier, but when he got there little remained. He could smell stoat around it. White Chin ate what he could salvage from the bones and feathers, pawed the ground with his front foot to show he was done and moved on, head lifted high as he scented the March air. It had a richness to it that had not been there through the winter months. He breathed deeply and set off at a wild gallop from the pure pleasure of being young and fit, through the wood to the edge of the moor. There were rabbits everywhere. His newfound boldness made him feel up to the challenge. Today he would catch a rabbit.

As he watched, hidden and downwind, he learned that their hearing was sharper even than his and that having their eyes on the sides of their heads seemed to let them see more easily in all directions. Their sheer numbers were a form of protection for them, as he became giddy just looking at them. Being an instinctive hunter he knew that stealth was everything, so he allowed his own eyes, nose, whiskers and ears to lead him to the entrance of a warren that seemed to lodge the biggest colony of rabbits. There he crouched above it, still as a stone, well concealed by undergrowth. Soon he was rewarded by action.

Two half-grown rabbit does came squeaking noisily up the main tunnel of their warren, pursued playfully by a young buck and the three of them burst out of the entrance beneath White Chin. He dived upon them and, as they scattered, he focussed on the middle one, grabbing her by the neck. He felt the enormous power of her hind legs as she tried to kick herself into freedom and he bit hard and deep into her spinal chord. It was done well and quickly and the rabbit was his. White Chin felt a surge of triumph at his success. He greedily started to eat. As he swallowed his third mouthful he stopped. This would be his gift to Adorabelle. He put the body down on the ground to get a better grip on it. He was a great distance from Lake House but he could smell Adorabelle on the wind and tell exactly how far away she was. Gripping the rabbit carcass between his teeth, he flung the bloody body over his shoulder so it rested on his back, then started to run through the trees towards the long-haired, green-eyed beauty who had captured his heart. He bounded through the dappled wood, not heeding who saw him with his swag.

As he reached the middle of the wood he stopped to adjust his burden and he saw a flash of white as Adorabelle came towards him. She mewed to him invitingly and danced towards him sideways. He dropped his present at her feet and they touched noses. He gently butted his trophy along the ground towards her, watching her. She sniffed it and licked it and he could see she was pleased with his gift. Both started to tear at the flesh and afterwards they groomed themselves and each other and started to play. They galloped wildly, zigzagging through the trees, watching each other out of the corners of their eyes. As their game developed Adorabelle became ever more skilful at hiding herself, teasing White Chin playfully. Although he couldn't stop her, it made him fretful.

And then it happened. One minute she was there, the next she was gone. White Chin ran, calling, to begin with playfully, but as his companion remained silent, with more concern. He charged back and forth, listening, mewling out for her. He stopped and heard her calling, distantly. Her voice rose higher in a shrill, seemingly endless scream of pain.

Adorabelle was thrashing around on the ground as he raced towards her. She kept pulling and tugging at something. Her eyes were wide and frightened. As he came close to her she spat at him in fear and pain. She tugged and heaved. She screamed again. White Chin was in despair. He tried to get close to her to lick her nose, but she would have none of it. She was terrified. White Chin stood back and looked on in horror. He could see part of a cruel wire wound around her thigh that she kept biting. He went closer to try to help but again she struck out at him in her agony.

White Chin stayed with her for some time, but in the end her distress upset him too much and he crawled slowly away. He could still hear her but he knew he couldn't get close enough to help. He started to move in the direction of Lake House until he could no longer hear Adorabelle's pitiful calls. As he moved out of earshot he changed his mind and retraced his steps. He timidly approached the injured cat. As he reached her he tried to touch her nose, but she hissed at him.

White Chin was confused. He couldn't understand how she was hurt and why she wouldn't move. Why wasn't she like she'd been before? He walked away again in a larger circle and once more found himself getting closer to Lake House. There was no one around but he hadn't forgotten the water jug that had been thrown at him during the night. Just then he heard the clatter of a horse's hooves. It was Kirstie on Buster. White Chin heard her call his name, but he had other things on his mind and ran back into the wood towards Adorabelle. Kirstie trotted after him along the main woodland path, but when White Chin turned off towards the place where the stricken cat lay, Kirstie couldn't follow. White Chin distantly heard her calling after him, and then the sound of Buster's hooves fading as she trotted on.

As White Chin arrived at the side of the wounded Adorabelle he found her in a much worse state than when he had left her. Thick red blood was now oozing from her leg. As he approached her he realised she had started to tear at the only part of her trapped leg that she could reach. She had been desperately trying to chew through the wire, but attacking her own leg had been all that she could manage. She whimpered in agony. Her eyes were heavy-lidded and glazed.

White Chin sniffed her nose and licked her ear and this time met no resistance. She was too weak. At last he understood. Adorabelle, his beautiful Adorabelle was seriously injured. He mewled helplessly at her but she was too weak to return any call. White Chin ran out towards the path, not knowing what to do or where to go. He heard the chink of Buster's bridle as the pony chewed on his bit and the little cat stopped in the middle of the path, waiting.

It was half-term and Kirstie, having tacked Buster up that morning, couldn't believe her luck in meeting White Chin like this. She hadn't set eyes on him since he had taken himself away from Stuart and Anna's house and here he was, just sitting in the middle of the path as if he was waiting for her! She hastily slid off Buster and looping his reins over a branch, she bent down to scoop White Chin up in her arms.

She murmured all sorts of sweet-nothings to him in an ecstasy of joy. Just holding him and breathing in the smell of the top of his head was amazing, but it was a pleasure that was short-lived. White Chin wriggled to get free, making an odd miaowing sound as he jumped down and started to walk away. He stopped once and looked back at Kirstie as if expecting her to follow him and then he wriggled and squirmed through the prickly undergrowth. Kirstie reluctantly followed.

'What are you up to? Are you trying to take me somewhere?' she grumbled. White Chin disappeared under ferns and branches. Kirstie had a great deal of trouble keeping up with him, but she struggled through the undergrowth. Suddenly White Chin came to a halt by a clump of bushes, and he stood looking down at a sodden pink mass. Kirstie looked and blinked and looked again. She opened her mouth and heard, as if from some other source than herself, a blood-curdling scream that seemed to go on and on.

The injured cat didn't move. She had bled heavily and now she lay flat and still. She looked close to death.

Her head was recognisably Adorabelle, but her body fur was completely unfamiliar from the smeared blood matted in it.

Kirstie bent down and looked closer. The cat's leg was almost fully severed from her body. Without any warning, Kirstie turned away to be violently sick . Once it was over she stood up, not daring to look back at Adorabelle, but the image in her mind of what she had seen made her retch once more. With a superhuman effort she looked again at the wounded cat, and through the fan of her spread fingers she saw White Chin licking Adorabelle's unconscious head over and over again. His grief-stricken tenderness brought new tears to her eyes.

Kirstie swung around and ripped her way back through the trees to the path where she had tethered Buster. Untying him, she sprang into the saddle and cantered off towards Lake House. She trotted round the courtyard shouting tearfully, but there was no reply, so she kicked the surprised Buster into another canter down the road and over the bridge in the direction of home to get help from her Mum and Dad. She burst into the farmyard as her Dad was returning on his quad bike. As he climbed off it, Kirstie hurled herself from Buster's back and grabbed her father by his jacket.

'Quick! I think she's nearly dead.'

'Who's nearly dead?'

'Kay's cat, Adorabelle. Please hurry!'

'Calm down, Kirstie. Panicking only makes it worse.'

Bit by bit Kirstie explained between her sobs what she thought must have happened and where the cat was lying. John called out to Joan, who at that moment came in sight with a basket of eggs over her arm. Joan took one look at Kirstie and flung her arms around her, basket and all. After calming her daughter down she took the pony's reins and led him away to his field.

By this time the Land Rover was loaded up and John nodded at Kirstie to get in. When they reached the woods, Kirstie led her father on foot to Adorabelle. When he saw how badly mangled she was, he cut the snare free from its anchor with his wire cutters, but left the wire around the leg so that she wouldn't lose any more blood than she had already. He laid the cat gently in the box, covering her with a towel and started to march back through the wood as quickly as he could. Kirstie had to run to keep up with him.

'Dad, will she be all right?' she panted.

'Not sure, she's lost a lot of blood. We don't have much time.'

As they drove past Lake House there was still no sign of Kay Keble – they would just have to tell her later what had happened. They were nearly at the vet's before Kirstie suddenly wondered what had happened to White Chin. Although her mind was full of poor Adorabelle, she had to admire that little black-and-white cat; he'd definitely used her to save Adorabelle. She must find him as soon as this was all over. There could be more traps out there.

From then on things moved with astonishing speed. Bill Smith, the vet, immediately examined the now unconscious cat before preparing to operate on her. Using long-pointed cutting pliers, he removed enough of the wire to reveal the awful depth of the wound. As he did this, Kirstie went pale, realising exactly how terrible the damage was. John, when he saw his daughter's sheet-white face, had escorted her out of the examination room, concerned that she might faint.

As Kirstie sat in the waiting room she thought about what the vet had said when he first looked at the snare. He had said they were technically legal, but not when they were anchored as this one had been. Such snares were completely undiscriminating in what animals they trapped and wounded. As a country vet he regularly had to perform amputations on domestic animals that had been caught in them. If he had his way they would be permanently banned. They were cruel and evil things. Dully Kirstie thought back to the carolling, remembering what Doug and Bernie had been saying. Why, oh why hadn't she warned Kay?

There had been a brief delay while they tried to contact Kay Keble and eventually John tracked her down on her mobile and got her to give Bill her agreement for an immediate amputation. Kirstie had asked her Dad how Kay had sounded when he told her what happened. He didn't say anything but just put both his thumbs down, shaking his head. As soon as

Kay had given the go-ahead, John had taken Kirstie's hand and led her out of the surgery on the grounds that now there was nothing more they could do and they would just have to wait for the results.

Later that evening, to Kirstie's huge relief, they received a good bulletin from Kay, who had spoken to Bill on the phone. Adorabelle was making excellent progress so far and there was no reason to assume she would not make a full recovery over time. The cat had been set up on a drip and was being closely monitored and fed with painkillers. She was to be kept in the surgery for twenty four hours and Kay would be allowed to collect her the day after tomorrow.

For the moment Adorabelle was 'out of it' and when she was allowed home she would need to be nursed very carefully indeed.

# 13

## And a time to lose

Kirstie had asked Kay if she could go with her to collect Adorabelle and Kay was more than happy to have company. It was only at the moment that they stepped into the vet's waiting room that Kirstie suddenly felt scared of what effect the horrors of the snaring and its aftershock might have on poor Adorabelle.

As the two of them were led into what the nurses called 'the ward', Adorabelle was lying in her cage with the legless side up. When Kirstie first saw the cat she froze. Somehow Adorabelle looked more butchered than she had imagined. She felt ashamed at her sense of disgust. She was surprised, although secretly relieved, when she heard Kay's unthinking expression of horror, as she first set eyes on her beloved cat. As Kay took in the whole picture her oaths became ever more colourful. In fact the young female cat had survived the ordeal surprisingly well and the vet nurse, whose duty it was to discharge the patient, assured them that Adorabelle had already been up and about and that she would be walking 'almost normally' before they knew what was happening. She told them that Bill had given her internal stitches to prevent her nibbling at them, and that she was fully dosed up with painkillers, which would need to be administered by Kay on a regular basis for the next few days.

When they got back to Lake House and gently removed Adorabelle from her cat carrier, the once-agile cat tried to stand up and instantly fell over. She miaowed pitifully and allowed herself to be carried over to her thick fluffy round rug. Kirstie sat with her, stroking her gently, while Kay clattered around in the kitchen.

Adorabelle lay quietly, with her bruised, swollen skin lying uppermost and her front paw covering her eyes, as if that would hide her from the world. Within five minutes, however, the cat had lifted up her head and using both her front legs had tried to turn around on her rug. Kay entered the room carrying cups of coffee. As she saw her darling cat struggling, she screwed up her face and shuddered slightly.

'Good Lord, Adorabelle! What on earth are you trying to do? Well come on then, if you're going to try to walk, let's see it! Show us what you're made of girl!'

Kirstie leaned forward to help the cat stand and Kay put out a restraining hand.

'Kirstie, stop that! You've got to let her be. Come on, let go of her. She's going to have to learn a new sense of balance from this day on.'

Kirstie was desperate to help Adorabelle walk, but Kay's voice had been firm, so she sat back and chewed her fingernails. The two of them observed Adorabelle begin her own private fight towards recovery. At first clumsily, and then with increasing confidence, the beautiful long-haired cat started to learn the new rules of how to lie down, stand and walk with three legs, on her own, unaided. Kirstie could hardly believe it and she hugged herself with pleasure. As Kay nursed her drink, she watched Adorabelle through narrowed eyes, but there was a gleam of pride in them.

'Atta girl, I knew you could do it!' They both watched the cat bravely countering the pain of her effort until it really was more than she could manage and she returned to her rug to sleep. But Adorabelle had triumphed.

Looking thoughtful, Kay leaned across and touched Kirstie's arm.

'D'you know I've never actually thanked you, Kirstie, for what you did out there. You . . .' she hesitated and then grinned sardonically at her young companion, 'you and that tuxedo cat of yours – so you claim – did a remarkable job saving poor Adorabelle's life. Bill told me on the phone that if she'd remained undiscovered much longer, she would almost certainly have died.' As Kay was finishing this sentence Kirstie flapped her hand in protest. She didn't want praise.

'No one could have left Adorabelle there like that, it was horrible. It was really scary. But . . . but it was hideous too.' She looked down at her hands and clenched her fists. 'I thought she *was* going to die,' she whispered quietly.

'Yes, I know. And if I get the so-and-so who put that snare there, he's going to die, or wish he was dead by the time I've finished with him. I'm going to sort that darned gamekeeper out, once and for all!'

Kirstie looked up at Kay in alarm. How could she possibly think that it was *Doug*? She stared at Kay, and as she did, a tiny nagging doubt entered the back of her mind. It was, she supposed, the sort of snare a gamekeeper *might* use.

'Don't look at me like that. It's bound to have been Doug. Who else would've done it? But listen Kirstie, don't you worry about that. This is my business.'

Kirstie swallowed hard and decided to change the subject. She really didn't want to get into the middle of this.

'I'm kind of worried about White Chin. Have you seen him since you got back? It really was him who tried to get help, honestly. I would never have found her or looked for her without him. And he obviously cared what happened to her.'

'No I haven't.' Kay got up and crossed the room

to put some music on. As she turned around she said, 'But I never told you, did I, that I chucked a jug of water over him the other night, because he was yowling to the moon like a mad thing?' She laughed. 'It worked though! He's been wonderfully quiet ever since.'

'Poor old White Chin!'

'Poor old White Chin, my foot. You should have heard him. It was enough to wake the dead. He went on and on and on.'

Kirstie giggled and started to collect her bits and pieces together, but she did think it had been rather beastly of Kay all the same. Now she had seen for herself how bravely Adorabelle was facing the challenges that lay ahead of her, she needed to establish, if she could, where poor White Chin was and how he was faring. She couldn't say anything to Kay, who was still reeling from what had happened to Adorabelle, but she was really scared White Chin might get snared himself.

Kirstie said her farewells to Kay and returned to the farm for her midday meal to find that everyone else had already eaten and that her food was warming in the oven. After telling her parents how brave Adorabelle was being, she then, a little nervously, launched into Kay's pronouncement about Doug. Her parents exchanged glances, but no one said anything.

'Don't you think she's wrong to blame Doug. About that snare I mean. After all she doesn't know anything definitely, does she?' Kirstie asked.

'Yes, that is worrying. It could have been poachers.

It could have been anyone. No one should ever level blame before they have definite proof,' said Joan.

'I know, but that's one of the weird things about Kay. She lets herself get all worked up. She's awful for it. Once she's made up her mind who's the villain, that's it.' As Kirstie said this, she felt a pang of guilt. Kay had given her support and love when Kirstie had felt the world was set against her and here she was, bad-mouthing her. Inside Kirstie felt quite cross with herself. Kay was a really good friend to her and friends didn't come perfectly formed, you took them 'warts and all', but the trouble with words slipping out of your mouth, is that you can't click 'undo'! Sighing she tossed her hair back off her shoulders and jumped up.

'Anyway I'm off to try to find White Chin. I'll go on Buster. Um, no I won't, I'll go on my bike, it'll be easier to find him that way.' Kirstie would never admit it to anyone, but she found the woods slightly scary on her own, on foot, and it felt somehow safer going through them if she was up on Buster's back. The business with the snare didn't make her feel any better either. But it was going to be easier to try to find White Chin on a bike, so there was nothing for it. She started to whistle as she cycled, which helped a bit.

Kirstie entered the trees from the track at the back of Lake House and cycled the full length of the wood until she got to the open moorland at the other end. She paused repeatedly, and called and whistled but there was no sign of anything. As she started on the long journey back towards Lake House she caught a brief glimpse of black and a flash of what might have been white socks disappearing between the trees. She threw her bike down and raced after the shadowy figure.

It was White Chin. He paused when he heard her calling and turned and looked at her over his shoulder. She begged and wheedled and flattered and pleaded, but White Chin blinked at her once and turned away. He looked like a cat who wanted his own company, and didn't mind Kirstie knowing that. Kirstie was gutted. Why wouldn't this little cat come to her?

She was sure he was fond of her and that there was a real bond, so what was it that was making him stay away from her? Was it as she feared – had he now really lost all trust in people after being thrown out by Stuart and Anna? She had one more go at approaching him but he got up, waving his tail in the air, and just melted away into the trees in the way that she knew too well. He didn't seem to want her near him. She picked up her bike, her heart heavy inside her, and slowly started to cycle home.

White Chin, in fact, didn't know at all what he should do, or where he should go. But his mind was focussed on his own kind. The only thing in the world he wanted was his beautiful cat-friend back. He wanted to see

Adorabelle. He wanted to play with her again and run and chase like they had before. He didn't know where she had gone, or if she was all right. All he knew was that the last time he had seen her, she had been ill.

White Chin hated the place where Adorabelle had become trapped. It frightened him. It was bad. But perhaps he should go back to it to see if there was some clue for him about where she was? He returned to the scene of the snaring and smelt every inch of the ground. And yes, there it was, that familiar scent from long ago. He knew that man's smell: it was a bad smell. As well as being on the main track, the smell was close to the snare.

There was, however, no recent smell of Adorabelle. All White Chin could find was her scent from when she had been trapped and had bled so badly. The last that he had seen of her was her being carried away in a box by Kirstie and her Dad. Instinct made White Chin feel that Adorabelle would return, if she could, to her home, so perhaps that was where he should wait for her.

White Chin started to walk in the direction of Lake House. But he walked slowly. He didn't at all like the pale-haired woman with the deep voice who lived with Adorabelle. She did nasty things to cats like throwing water and shouting. He had spent the last two nights in the woods but he hadn't found any good shelter and it was cold at night out in the open. He decided to risk the hot-headed woman who lived here and return to the house to see if he might find his lovely Adorabelle.

As he approached Lake House he smelled Kirstie again. But of Adorabelle there was no scent anywhere. He returned to the shed to sleep uneasily on the crumpled dustsheets.

# 14

## Rejection – again!

In the early morning White Chin went into the woods and made a breakfast out of three worms and a mouse, but on his return there was still no fresh scent of his Adorabelle. He stationed himself between the house and the studio where he could view any comings or goings through the front door without being seen. Nothing happened for an age. He snoozed on and off and then he heard the shouty woman addressing someone or something.

As he watched, well concealed, the woman opened the door. More time passed and then he saw her, Adorabelle, standing in the doorway, sniffing the air. She walked forward into the garden. Her movements were different and she seemed timid. White Chin made his tomcat greeting to her and she lifted her head in his direction, but although she looked at him, her mind was on other things.

White Chin walked towards her. As he got near her he could see the cruel wound and naked skin where her back leg had once been. He stopped as he caught her smell. That was the trouble; it *wasn't* her smell. It was the smell of the after-effects of the chemicals used during the operation but all White Chin knew was that it wasn't how Adorabelle *should* smell and he hated it, so he hissed at her. Startled, she shrank back from him. White Chin was confused so he approached her again. As he neared Adorabelle it was the same wrong smell, so again he hissed. Adorabelle turned around and limped back into the house and White Chin retreated under cover. A little while later Kay came to the door but, seeing nothing, she returned inside, closing the front door behind both of them.

White Chin loitered around Lake House for the rest of that day but never saw any more of Adorabelle. He spent the night in the shed but before sunrise he was out on watch again. As the sun shone the temperature rose and it became a warm spring day and White Chin felt hopeful. Soon the front door was flung wide and left open and as White Chin watched he saw Adorabelle approach. She seemed to have more confidence and walked forward without stopping. White Chin approached her, but as he got near to her this time, to his dismay, she hissed at him. She still had the strange vet smell on her, but it was less strong and he could now recognise her old familiar scent at last. He moved towards her again, but she turned her back to him. He stood still.

Adorabelle walked the length of the building and disappeared around the end of the barn. White Chin, curious to know what she was doing, followed her at a distance. She approached a large bushy tree and stood at its base looking up. Slowly and with care, using the claws in her front feet and her tail to steady her, the three-legged cat half walked and half climbed up its lower branches, moving with great skill from one branch to the next, until she reached a spot about three feet above ground where she stopped and surveyed the world around her. She was firmly balanced on her front legs, holding herself in place with her right rear leg, apparently totally unworried by the absence of a leg on the other side.

At that point White Chin heard Kay calling out and he slunk quickly out of sight. Kay came round the building and Adorabelle directed a small high-pitched miaow of mock alarm at her. Kay immediately looked up and saw her precious cat amidst the branches. She spoke to Adorabelle in a low voice and cajoled her along the branch and into her arms. Adorabelle was facing White Chin over Kay's shoulder as she was carried back to the house and he heard her purring loudly. She caught his eye, stared at him coldly and stopped purring. Turning her head away from him towards Kay she resumed her loud purring and lavishly licked Kay's hair.

White Chin stayed where he was for a little time thinking about this rejection and then he moved off towards the woods, his tail and head hung low. He spent an hour hunting and killed a small rabbit which he ate in one go.

White Chin was confused and hurt. Adorabelle hadn't been the same since she had been caught in the snare. She had been his friend and he wanted her to stay that way, but it was to be no more, it seemed. There was no point in his remaining here. White Chin walked through the gates of Lake House and over the bridge. He passed by Old Bridge Farm where he stood briefly on one side of the cattle grid looking at the red bike propped against the inside wall, and then he resumed his journey. After he passed the wall of the farm, he left the road and went into the field where he had first discovered the river bank. Loneliness weighed on him and each footprint he made as he retraced his tracks along every wall and through every hedge made him sadder. When he had travelled the other way, all those days ago, he had been so full of hope and excitement. Now High Fell Wood was calling to him again, to resume the life of a solitary male. He would live without cats and without people. None could be trusted.

Kirstie cycled up to Lake House as soon as she got back from school, longing to see how the three-legged patient had got on and also hoping she might find White Chin somewhere nearby. She was greeted by an excited Kay who was full of Adorabelle's achievements. She walked Kirstie around the back of the barn and showed her the bush where Adorabelle had climbed.

'When my beautiful Adorabelle was a kitten she started to use that as her climbing frame. Well somehow, I don't know how, she managed it today, and she went halfway up it!' As Kay said this there was a slight catch in her voice.

Kirstie looked up at the American quickly and replied, 'At the vet's they said that cats can recover really quickly, but I never thought she would be up and about like this already. It's really brilliant! So she will be OK, you'll see!' And she gave Kay a little hug.

Back in the house Adorabelle was lying stretched out in state on the sofa and Kay almost whispered, 'Yes. She is one brave girl.' As she said this, she combed Adorabelle's huge plumed tail gently between her fingers, with obvious affection. Kirstie watched this with a strange sort of envy, wishing she could find 'her' cat. She got up to leave knowing that her tea awaited her back at the farm, vowing to herself that she would come back and look for him properly.

When Kirstie arrived home she found her mother and father talking about a diary story which had just been published in that week's *Gazette*. Her Dad started to read it out. The piece quoted an internationally renowned 'sculptress' – Kay of course – who lived at the old cornmill on the Troonholme Park Estate. She had told the reporter, "the time has come to stop local gamekeepers placing illegal snares for foxes. Snares which do untold harm to innocent domestic pets. My own Maine Coone queen was nearly killed in one just a few days ago."

Kirstie peered over her Dad's shoulder to see a glamorous photograph of Kay, holding Adorabelle, legless side up, on her knee. Her Mum groaned and shook her head, sighing. Kay going to the local press in this way would just cause trouble. Joan said it was plain wrong to accuse 'the gamekeepers' in this way, unless of course she had proof that they didn't know about. John said they knew that Doug was innocent because Doug had shown them both where a more recent snare had been placed. Kirstie wanted to know where, but Dad just told her that as long as she stayed on the main path through the woods she would be OK and she didn't need to know. This knowledge made her shiver, but as soon as she had gulped down her tea she headed off back to the woods, mumbling to her parents that she had forgotten something.

Kirstie then started a systematic search through Troonholme Park for White Chin. She was a bit scared because she realised that if someone was out and about placing snares, it would almost certainly be when it was dark and dusk was falling now. But she was determined to find the little cat who had so powerfully captured her heart. She called again and again but there was no sign of him anywhere. She went around the back of Lake House and found the old shed with the broken door. The door was padlocked but she peered for what seemed ages through the window. In the gloom she couldn't see anything, except old pots and a pile of yellow dustsheets which glowed slightly in the dusk. No evidence of any cat could be seen. He must be here somewhere, surely?

Kirstie chewed her lip. She felt as if she was never going to find her little cat and she was sure that what he really needed was love and affection and a proper warm home. But at least she hadn't seen any snares.

It was quite dark when she finally gave up. At last, turning her back on the stone shed, she mounted her bike and cycled home. Troonholme Park definitely felt less friendly than it had before.

## 15

## Up the wet wild trees

White Chin settled back into his old territory in a mean mood. He felt out of sorts and discontented with life. The full richness of spring was bursting around him with a noisy vigour that he found tedious. He no longer felt part of it and it annoyed him. Discovering Adorabelle had been the most wonderful awakening to all that might be possible in his world, and now she had made it clear that she wanted no more of him. It was the first time in his life that he had been rejected by his own kind and although her scent was no longer near him, thoughts of her still haunted him.

He found his old cave and quickly made it clear to a young hedgehog who had thought it rather a good home, that it wasn't – at any rate, not for him! He checked out his regular drinking places and his best hunting sites and scent marked widely, so that no woodland creature might be in any doubt that the feline predator had returned.

Time passed and White Chin began to hunt on High Fell with a new zeal. He had become deadly efficient. He caught young rabbits as a matter of course. Their numbers were increasing daily and he found the kits, bobbing around in their carefree way, almost insultingly easy to catch. White Chin became stronger and more wily with each passing day and proved himself to be the unchallenged king of his jungle. That is, until the night of the lamping.

Late one evening, White Chin, who had been waiting for the darkness of true night, woke up in his cave feeling hungry. Hunting was easier in the darkest hours, for then the rabbits were at their most active as they ate and played. He crept out and stationed himself near the drinking pool, which he had found to be a good place to select and kill his prey. He had to take especial care to conceal himself there as the woodland monitors, such as the watchful rooks and blackbirds of daylight hours or the gimlet-eyed owls of night, were devils for alerting other creatures that there was an active predator about. Once that happened there was nothing for it but to move to another hunting ground.

White Chin, to his irritation, heard the owls hooting their alarm calls, although he had been so careful not to be seen. And then it happened. Suddenly the whole woodland was filled with noise and light and everything changed. There was the sound of a 4x4 vehicle revving up its engine as it crashed its way through the undergrowth and as White Chin looked across he saw the beams of powerful lamps shining and turning up and down and in between trees. There were human voices. A woman's voice and harsh male shouts. And there were dogs. Two lurchers who ran along the length of the beams. Then in the light from the torches he saw the two dogs grab the back leg of a roe buck and sink their teeth into it. The deer screamed out in pain as the dogs brought it to the ground.

White Chin shrank back into the undergrowth for cover, but the voices became louder and more excited. There were repeated popping sounds, like small explosions. The screams continued. And then more voices and more lights. A loud bang and silence. There were sounds of men shouting at each other and cursing and then chopping noises. White Chin smelt blood and crept forward to watch. Through the trees he could see a group of men and a woman standing around the body of a young roe stag. An older man stepped forward and shouted out in a harsh, excited voice. White Chin shrank back, his pupils dark from fear. He knew that voice and that smell!

One of the men was cutting through the neck of the stag and there was blood everywhere. White Chin was about to move away when suddenly the spotter, a young man with a lamp standing on the back of the Jeep, shone the bright light straight into his eyes.

'Quick, quick. A fox. Go get it!' he yelled.

'You squint-eyed little toe-rag – you're barking mad,' the older man shouted back.

At that moment someone released the dog and White Chin had a brief glimpse of a thin grey lurcher, tongue lolling from the side of his mouth, bounding straight for him. White Chin ran like a scared rabbit, in a wild zigzag and, claws ready to grip, he leaped for the shaggy trunk of a tall Scots Pine. He scrambled higher and higher, until he found a branch a good twenty feet off the ground, where he sat, tense and alert. A light shone up from below, blinding him and he heard the sound of laughter.

'Here, isn't that your cat?' a younger man asked, in a voice that White Chin recognised.

'Nah, that ain't no cat of mine – it belongs to the woods now,' the big man replied. 'Come on, let's get on with the job in hand, and stop messin' about.' And he spat violently in White Chin's direction.

The lurcher sat at the bottom of the tree staring up aggressively at White Chin. The little cat stayed where he was. He was taking no chances. The lamping party continued to disrupt the wood for a further hour, but eventually they had cut up the deer to their satisfaction and put the pieces in plastic boxes in their Jeep. The dogs were ordered into a big cage in the back and with much slamming of doors and cursing they drove off.

When the wood finally fell quiet again White Chin edged his way back down the trunk and returned to ground level. He heard something crunching on bone and as he scented the air, the strong waft of badger reached him. He looked through the trees and could see the outline of a large boar badger rummaging amongst the severed limbs of the deer. It was time to move on.

White Chin needed somewhere to hide. He crept off into the high wood and found the cavern that he knew had been the badger sett when he had lived here before. Outside the cavern entrance were the remains of rabbit carcasses and mice. It was quite altered from how it had been before; it was now untidy and smelly. He slowly entered the long airless tunnel. He could hear the mewling of young. The smell of fox was overpowering.

Although White Chin had been looking for a hidey-hole, curiosity now possessed him and without considering the consequences, he slowly edged his way down the ramp. As he entered the chamber, he was dimly aware of a nest of young cubs. They made little mewling sounds and the pong was suffocating. He sat quietly watching the cubs, twitching his tail. All of a sudden he felt the most terrible pain as needle sharp teeth sank into the flesh at the base of his spine. It felt as if something was eating him alive, just above his tail. He swung around with a scream and found himself facing an angry vixen.

The fox had her ears flat back against her head and

her teeth gleamed white in the dark, stained with White Chin's blood. She yickered in a rising scream at him. The sound made his heart stop and he shrank back against the far wall in fear.

He had been mad to enter what had become a foxes' den containing young cubs and he knew that he had to get out and quickly. His fur had puffed up around him in fear but it gave him the appearance of huge size and his claws were unsheathed and mean-looking. Instinctively he hissed and the sound was like water hitting hot coals. The vixen continued to scream threats at him and all her teeth were fiercely bared as she closed in on him. He could feel the force of her breath as she spat in his face. White Chin gave one more tremendous hiss to hold her at bay and legged it as fast as he could into the open air.

He was bleeding deeply and the pain was fierce and throbbing. He wanted to find somewhere safe to hide away and lick his wound, but leaving a trail of blood was unwise. Some distance from the sett he found a sheltered hollow under the drooping bough of an ash tree and he licked and licked, but the bleeding continued. The bite had been savage and deep. The pain was so great that he purred a little to try to make himself feel better. It didn't work. He felt sore and the pain made him fearful. He felt too weak to get back to his cave and he needed to eat.

Slowly and painfully he started to retrace his steps to where the stag had been slaughtered as there would be a ready meal awaiting him and he was in no state to hunt. He found the bits of leg and head, or what remained of them after the badger had had his fill, and he ate a little, but his appetite had gone.

White Chin crept to a hollow under a bramble bush and curled up to sleep. Later that night, he had a strange disturbed nightmare about being chased by a scary creature who started out in his dream looking like a giant rabbit, but who slowly turned into a smelly fox. His legs twitched in a dreaming run and the pain from his deep flesh wound woke him up. He had a dry mouth and felt feverish but he had to force himself to get up and find water to drink. He returned feeling dizzy and unwell before falling into a fitful sleep, aware beyond anything else of the throbbing pain at the base of his tail.

As he slept and woke feverishly he reflected on the events of the night. In doing so, White Chin expanded his list of most-hated woodland creatures, in which badgers already ranked, to include men, women, lurchers and, in particular, foxes.

# 16

## To weep

In the early dawn White Chin was disturbed by a strange animal call from the copse nearby. It was high, almost a scream. As he rose up to investigate he saw a bright chestnut roe buck sniffing the ground where last night's deer had been so savagely slaughtered. The buck's flank quivered as he scented the ruin. He lifted his head and turned his soft gaze upon the cat. His eyes looked like dark liquid pools. He snorted and shook his antlers, striking the ground with his dainty hoof, then he turned and with a mighty bound jumped away between the trees.

Some hours later White Chin woke again to hear a dog barking. He knew that bark! And that scent. The dog passed him, not interested in him or his hiding place, intent on something else. Shortly afterwards the little cat heard a quad bike. He slept again and woke to hear three voices. These were gentle and there was no shouting as there had been last night.

John Metcalfe was talking to Doug and Bernie Wilcock. They were grouped around the trampled area where the stag had been slain. All that now remained of the roe deer since the various woodland creatures had joined in the plunder were three hooves with small amounts of shin bone attached and the head. The ground was dark with the blood spilled the night before and traces of the butchering were everywhere. It had been Shep who had in fact discovered the slaughter, when he was supposed to be moving sheep. He had found the deer's remains just too tempting to ignore and had had to be called abruptly to order as John used his mobile to call in the gamekeepers, having seen the widespread evidence of a raiding vehicle.

John now picked up one of the bloody hooves and turned it over in his hands.

'Doug, I know that High Fell is well off your patch, but given the snaring problems you have been having down in Troonholme Park do you think this could be connected?' He puffed out his cheeks in exasperation, running his fingers through his hair adding, 'I suppose what I'm asking is . . . do you think it's the same gang who've been putting those illegal snares round your way? You know, like that one that caught Kay's cat?'

Doug and Bernie both looked puzzled.

'To be honest, John, I haven't got a clue,' Doug said. 'That snare could have caught anything at all: rabbit, dog, badger, fox, stoat or even a mink. I imagine it was set for a fox, but who by and why? Since then we've found another one, newly laid. I wanted to see if it felt like the same hand. I really don't like someone messing on my patch.'

Bernie added, 'This is the third time already this spring that there's been signs of deer poaching around here. And the police we've talked to reckon it's a gang selling them off to restaurants and pubs. Venison is more and more popular these days. roe deer won't fetch as much as red deer, but there are plenty about of course.' Bernie squatted down to inspect the grisly remains and peered up at her husband, questioningly.

'So what do we think killed it then?'

Doug lifted the butchered head and studied it carefully.

'If I had to guess I would say a .22 rifle. They don't need a licence and they only make a quiet pop when they go off. It's a bad gun to use on a deer, but there's no control over poachers. And from the look of it, they used lurchers to get it in the beam. That's not clever.'

They fell silent and then Doug joked feebly. 'At least Kay Keble can't blame this one on us!'

'She's trouble that one. She's putting it about that we tried to murder her cat. I mean, as if . . . ' Bernie tutted. Throughout this conversation White Chin had been slipping in and out of consciousness as a fever raged through his body from his septic wound, and he had heard the voices rising and falling as if in a dream. He now heard the quad bike firing up and Shep barking excitedly in his direction. The cat cowered down, unable to run or hide. The quad bike stopped and he saw John walking towards him. With great difficulty White Chin stood up to try to walk away and he heard the man gasp out. White Chin fell over and nearly lost consciousness, then he felt a pair of strong, rough hands holding him and a jacket was wrapped about him. He was being lifted up and placed gently in the back of the sheep trailer. White Chin raised his head to try to see what Shep was doing. The dog was sitting on the seat behind John, facing the other way. White Chin put his head down again, gratefully.

The little cat felt himself rattling around in his section of the trailer as it banged down the track from the wood, but he felt so poorly now that he was prepared to put up with anything. He had no strength left and he just wanted to sleep. As he closed his eyes, he heard Shep's conversational barks as if they were coming from a great way off.

On their arrival at Old Bridge Farm, John carried White Chin into the kitchen and laid him on the floor still wrapped in his jacket. John called upstairs to his daughter.

'Hey, come and see what I've got down here!'

Kirstie's pleasure and shock at seeing the little wounded cat was so great that she burst into uncontrollable sobs. Joan came forward and slowly prized her daughter off White Chin, suggesting that as he was very ill some rest and peace might be a good idea. She bustled around and found an old bed that really belonged to Dilly, their black Bengal rescue cat, and settled him down by the side of the Aga stove. Joan looked at the wound and pulled a face as she tweezered off the three maggots that were weaving around the raw site. She bathed the wound with warm water and antiseptic, and White Chin patiently put up with it all. His eyes kept closing – he was clearly unwell. Joan asked Kirstie to keep an eye on him, for which she needed little encouragement. The cat slept solidly all day and ate nothing. By early evening it was decided that he should go to the vet's.

John took them down in the Land Rover, with Kirstie holding the cat carrier next to her to stop it rocking about and so she could talk to White Chin through the bars. He miaowed out weakly. It was the first cat carrier he had ever been in, and he hated it. He wasn't that keen on the movement and noise of the Land Rover either. At the vet's he was closely examined and injected with a large dose of antibiotic, his wound was cleaned again and then, to his absolute disgust, he was made to wear a large plastic 'Elizabethan' collar to stop him trying to lick his sore place. On the homeward journey he was held firmly on Kirstie's knee because his E-collar meant he wouldn't fit into the carrier. Although it was good to be free of the carrier, he still wailed in a surprisingly high falsetto voice all the way back to the farm.

When they arrived home Kirstie proudly carried him into their big warm kitchen and put him back on the old cat bed by the stove. She urged him to eat a tiny amount of food and drink some milk, but White Chin felt ill and he didn't like the unfamiliar collar around his neck. It was scary and annoying. He lowered his head, nose pressed into the bed which smelt strongly of Dilly, and his eyes slowly closed as he fell into a dreamless sleep.

## Cat civil war

White Chin slept soundly through the night and in the morning he felt a little better. When he woke he tried to stand, but his fever had left him with wobbly legs and he collapsed back on his cat bed.

The day had started early and White Chin was finding his new surroundings anything but restful. There was a lot of coming and going. Doors were opened and banged shut. John either talked to him or stroked him every time he passed, which White Chin found unsettling. He kept turning around trying to put his back to it all, but the big plastic collar round his neck upset him and where he had been bitten was sore and itchy.

As John opened the door from the kitchen into the yard for the third time, a blast of cold air blew in and White Chin huddled closer to the stove for heat. John pulled the door shut after him, but the latch didn't hold and it blew back open. With some difficulty White Chin got up from where he lay and shuffled across to the door. He peered outside and watched John open a barn across the yard and release Shep from the chain which held him. White Chin looked on, warily. He didn't trust Shep and couldn't tell what he might do. As he watched, the dog wandered off and drank, slurpily, from a puddle. He then cocked his leg for so long that he nearly fell over. White Chin shivered in the chilly wind and returned to his bed.

Although Shep wasn't supposed to go into the house, he would always grab the chance to make an entrance if it came his way. Seeing the farmhouse door ajar, he sidled over and shoved it hard with his shaggy wet head. It opened wide. He wiggled into the room in a sort of doggy dance of ecstasy, giving little furtive squeals of pleasure. As soon as he spied White Chin he opened his mouth and yapped in a friendly way. This scared the living daylights out of the cat who hissed back at him loudly. Shep blinked at that greeting but then looked around him to see if there was any food. Seeing nothing he returned his gaze to White Chin and panted at him amiably, turned tail and walked out of the house past a sleek black Bengal cat, tail high, looking like she had something on her mind.

Dilly had been aware that there was a strange cat in the house but the humans had stopped her going into the kitchen so that White Chin would be left in peace. By morning her curiosity got the better of her. Having heard the commotion she had climbed out of the open bathroom window at the back of the house and half walked, half slid down the slanting drainpipe until she landed in the field and was able to pad around to the front. She now sauntered in through the front door, skilfully dodging Shep's long dribbly tongue. Without a trace of hesitation she walked straight up to where White Chin lay.

He sat up to face her, feeling both awkward and not a little foolish in his Elizabethan Collar. She sat down a foot in front of him and stared across at him in complete silence.

White Chin had never in his life been stared at in this way. It was penetrating and challenging. He felt dismayed by it. He recoiled from her and hissed several times over, but the jet-black cat didn't move a muscle and her clear green eyes stayed focussed on White Chin's face without a blink. Licking his nose, he looked about him for an escape route.

As White Chin glanced towards the door he saw the outline of another cat passing outside. The outside cat stopped and stared back. They held each other's eyes in a neutral manner, while their noses twitched inquiringly. White Chin was looking at Stubs, an old war-torn tabby cat, whose stubby half-tail gave witness to one of his many hard-won battles from long ago. He was the farm cat and he lived in the outbuildings where he ruled the roost. Dilly took the opportunity, at White Chin's loss of concentration, to edge closer to him. Without delaying any longer the old farm cat continued silently on his way.

There was a loud kerfuffle and some very noisy bang, bang, banging down the stairs. The door from the hallway burst open and in walked Alex, Kirstie's younger brother. As he entered, White Chin's nervous, long, drawn-out hissing progressed to a defensive growl. His ears had flattened inside his collar and his whiskers had drooped right down. Dilly stared at him now even more intensely. Very slowly and deliberately she lowered herself onto her stomach and crept ever closer.

'Wayhay! Cat civil war. Brilliant!' Alex called out mischievously up the stairs behind him.

The result was electrifying. Almost immediately there was the sound of thundering feet banging down two flights of stairs, followed by Kirstie bursting into the kitchen as if she had been fired from a rocket, desperate to stop whatever was happening. She rushed over to White Chin, who had tried to back under a chair, but failed because of his big collar, and she glared down at Dilly. Dilly stopped crawling like a reptile and now turned her head casually to one side as if she had been doing nothing at all and blinked meekly, giving out a conversational miaow.

'How could you let Dilly in here? You knew that Mum said they were to be kept apart, beast!'

'Keep your shirt on, Stee, I didn't do anything, and you shouldn't jump to conclusions all the time.'

Kirstie snorted and gently tickled the little collared cat under his white chin. He slowly closed his eyes, able to relax now Dilly had turned her stare away from him.

'You're bad, you are,' Alex continued. 'You're always accusing *other* people of blaming the wrong person too soon and then you just go ahead and blame *me*. No idea how she got here. Was she in last night?'

'Yeah. She was. She was upstairs all night, so ner-ner-ne-ner-ner!' Kirstie sang and put her thumb on her nose, waving her fingers at Alex rudely. He grinned and shrugged his shoulders.

'Oh well, maybe she flew down then, or YER – I've got it. . .' He slapped his thigh laughing. 'Maybe she para-glided out of a window!'

Kirstie glared at her younger brother, turned away to give her full attention to the little black-and-white cat. As she continued to stroke White Chin he looked up at her and purred. He desperately wanted her to take away his nasty E-collar. It was irritating him and his wound itched – and he wasn't at all sure about this place. There was a lot going on. Kirstie stroked the fur along the length of his body, and White Chin arched his back, hoping she would scratch him near the itchy bit, but instead she bent down and just looked at the base of his tail.

'Your wound looks like it's healing – it's beginning to form a nice scab now, White Chin. Soon you'll be a better boy. I'll go and find you some breakfast.' And with that she wandered off towards the fridge and the cupboards to see what she could find, yanking up the waistband of her pyjama bottoms so she didn't trip over them. She came back with a bowl of cat kibble for White Chin and a bowl of cereal for herself. She put the cat bowl down on a small footstool so, raised off the ground, it was easier for White Chin to eat. Dilly watched all this from across the room and as White Chin started to eat she made a loud complaint in a basso meow. White Chin, who had been eating slowly because his collar made it difficult, stopped, alarmed.

Kirstie produced a plate of food for Dilly, which she plonked in front of her, while Joan came down and hauled out eggs and bacon from the fridge as she started preparing breakfast. She took a large mouthful of tea from her mug and as she swallowed it she looked across the room at her daughter, thoughtfully.

'Kirstie you do know that it may not work out for White Chin having him here with the other animals and he may want to go back to the woods again.'

'Oh Mum, no! Now he's here he'll be ever so happy, won't you White Chin?' And she bent down and flipped his big E-collar with her fingernails so it rattled, which made White Chin blink. He looked up at her questioningly.

'Go on, boy! You'll be happy, happy, happy, won't

you? Say yes!' She pulled the collar up and down to make him seem as if he was nodding. He gave a little mew in protest.

'Kirstie that isn't fair. I don't think he's enjoying that! And you do need to make a fuss of him you know. He clearly hates being collared in that way. I'm afraid that Dilly isn't helping either. She's such a madam the way she always has to be top cat.'

'I *was* making a fuss of him, before you walked in, honestly. Look! See! I've already fed him!'

Joan laughed at the expression of outraged innocence on the face of her daughter and now changed the subject. Lambing was in full swing, and it was the time of year when everyone on the farm had to muck in. As Joan bustled around the kitchen talking over her shoulder Kirstie nodded her head happily to the request that she and Alex put in as many hours as they could give, especially around feeding time, up in the lambing sheds now that the holidays had started.

At Joan's request, Kirstie rushed upstairs to get dressed and came down still pulling her clothes on to bang out of the front door and tell her father that breakfast was ready. She ran round the back of the farmhouse towards the shed holding the lambing pens, where she found her father bending over one of the ewes, grunting and heaving as he tugged at the protruding front legs of a lamb reluctant to leave its mother's womb. As she watched, he pulled away a long body in a slimy birth sac that he gently laid on the ground in front of its panting mother, who quickly started to nibble and lick at it. Within seconds the lamb's head was clear of the sac and it was bleating and already struggling to get on its feet.

As Kirstie watched her father handling the ewe she felt the sense of wonder that she always had whenever she witnessed a birth. She often thought how awful it must be for the lamb when it was nearly time to be born, being scrunched up in the dark, all tight inside its mother. There you are, with no room to move but warm and safe and then the next minute there's some horny-handed old farmer hauling you out by your front feet. Or maybe worse you get born on your own and land up in a deep pile of freezing cold wet snow. Kirstie hugged herself at the thought. And the miracle then was how within seconds these tiny shivering lambs would get on their feet and find their mother's milk – and sometimes their mothers, especially new ones, weren't much help, either.

While Kirstie daydreamed away her father was busy bent double over the lamb he had just delivered, spraying its naval with some bright orange antiseptic liquid. The lamb's mother bleated her concern and nuzzled her new babe possessively.

John stood up, stretching his sore back and grinned down at his daughter. She looked up at him. Yesss, this was as good a moment as any to work on him.

'Dad, I forgot. Breakfast's ready . . .' She paused, and then in her most wheedling and persuasive voice she went on, 'White Chin can stay, can't he, please, please?'

'Oh, Kirstie. Now he's here I expect he can stay.' He sighed and grinned sheepishly at her.

'But look here, you need to clear it with your mother, you know? Remember – now he is your responsibility and you have to take proper care of him . . .'

'I will, I will. Dad – you know I will. I promise!' Kirstie was so thrilled she wanted to dance. At last, her dream had come true! White Chin could stay!

Over the next few days life began to improve for White Chin. His injury continued to itch and he constantly wanted to lick it as it started to heal, but his hated plastic collar was removed the following day, which helped restore his shaken confidence in this difficult household. The medication from the vet worked and his fever left him.

Now he was able to move around freely amongst the other animals and feel equal. Getting on with them was complicated, but although there was a lot of jostling for position, no blood was shed. The huge pleasure for White Chin in this new domesticated existence was that Kirstie, able to enjoy the freedom of home life during the Easter holidays, spent long hours talking to him, stroking him, sitting near him, carrying him and grooming him, and he adored the attention. For the first time since being a small kitten someone really seemed to care about him. Kirstie liked to cradle him on his back, and although at the beginning he hadn't much cared for it, he learned quite soon to enjoy it. He loved it when she put her finger in his upturned paw and he could cup it by gently holding it in his pad. As he purred he would dribble with pleasure.

The best thing of all was that most nights Kirstie would come and carry him up to her room in her arms when she was going to bed. Once there, he was able to paddle himself a comfortable place, safely curled up behind the crook of her knees. On a couple of occasions he had been outside hunting and had missed her bedtime and on his return had attempted to creep round the ever-vigilant Dilly who kept permanent watch on the landing sofa, but it was quite impossible to get past her. If he tried to pass her, she would first stare and then attack, so he would have to stay out of the way and wait until morning for Kirstie's company again.

Life on the farm was lived at a helter-skelter rate and people and animals were permanently bustling to and fro. During the Easter holidays the two children were as good as their word and both of them laboured hard on the farm. Kirstie spent long hours in the lambing sheds helping her father and mother with the rush of newborn lambs, and at others she would be out on Buster, mindful of her mother's concerns for him.

Alex too put in a good hand's turn and now he was allowed, whenever possible, he would try to persuade his Dad to let him drive his tractor off-road. His current pride and joy however was his new buck rabbit, who had recently fathered his first litter of six 'kits', as Alex insisted everyone call them.

All this activity encouraged White Chin to poke his nose into everything and soon he had thoroughly investigated all the farm buildings. He watched the goings-on around the lambing sheds with interest and learned that sheep, both old and new, were no threat to a cat, although lambs liked to play and could be quite bouncy and rough. As they got bigger they weren't above chasing a cat, which they seemed to think was rather fun. Sometimes a ewe with a baby lamb would stamp her foot at him warningly, but it never amounted to anything, and he learned to keep his distance from the newborns.

He found the big wire enclosure which contained Alex's rabbits. He understood that these rabbits were different from woodland ones, but in the main he saw little of them, as they seemed to stay in their shed out of the wind and rain. He checked them from time to time, but they never went anywhere. He found them mildly interesting. Rabbit was, after all, rabbit and there were quite a lot of them.

There were hens too. He had found the hens on the second morning after his collar came off. He had followed Dilly out of the house and she had gone into the long polytunnel, which was at the end of the hen coops. When Joan let the hens out in the morning, she always threw down seed for them; immediately wild chaffinches and tits would fly in. Dilly was simply waiting for her chance to get a small bird breakfast.

White Chin watched Dilly, but he didn't join in. He had thought she was after the hens but they were big birds and he decided they would be too difficult to catch. She was after smaller fry.

The blight in all of this otherwise pleasant farm life for White Chin was Dilly. She rarely dropped her territorial guard. As soon as the door was opened in the morning she had to race out first and roll all over the ground, scent marking everything. If White Chin rubbed himself against anything, then she had to go up and rub over where he had rubbed so her scent was strongest. She was the only female cat he had seen regularly spraying. On many occasions when John parked up his quad bike Dilly would smell the tyres for minutes on end and then make small mewling noises, before spraying them with a loud hiss. White Chin found her habits perplexing and didn't feel altogether at ease in her presence. She seemed to want to assert her dominance over him at every possible opportunity and her stare freaked him out!

He was also pretty wary of Stubs. Stubs had an amazingly tough look in his eye, which White Chin would glimpse as he passed by, but for the moment at least it seemed that Stubs was happy to live and let live as long as White Chin gave him space. White Chin was especially careful that he didn't scent mark Stubs's favourite haunts in the barns.

So the cat rules became defined in White Chin's head. Inside the house it felt to him that the territory was pretty firmly held by Dilly. Outside wasn't much better, as there Stubs seemed to claim everything.

And on top of the feline hierarchy, there was the added complication of Shep. White Chin's problem was that he had never before met a dog at close quarters, and his instinct told him they were the enemy, although he could tell in his heart that Shep was gentle and held no malice for him. Truth was, he wasn't good to be near. He was so noisy! Not only that he was also bouncy, smelly and usually wet. And there was the tongue – a great dribbling skateboard of a tongue, and he almost never put it away!

# 18

## What might be the equal or even the sequel to those sheep in the treacle?

As the Easter holidays passed, White Chin began to feel a sense of peace and belonging that had, up to this moment, been missing from his young feral life. He no longer felt the call of the wild in the way he had when he felt himself reined in at Stuart and Anna's house. Here he could sense the fierce intensity with which Kirstie loved him and it made him feel safe. He felt a strong bond with this little girl. Her home felt the right place for him to be. These emotions more than made up for his dread of Dilly's frequent challenges and Stubs's scornful pretence that he didn't exist. He had learned to ignore Shep and to take ducking action to avoid the always-present tongue.

White Chin was beginning now to enjoy the rhythms of the farm, which was its own world. In spite of this, he would still take himself off hunting in Troonholme Park, it being the nearest woods to the farm, but he rarely stayed away at night.

Sometimes too he would seek out the company of Adorabelle. Frequently she wanted to have little to do with him, but being a nosey young tomcat he liked to keep track of her scent as she moved around the locality of Lake House. By this means he would know where she was and what she was up to and even what mood she might be in. On occasion she would touch noses with him and they would spend a few minutes together, which gave him great pleasure. But he could never be sure how welcoming she might be.

Kirstie would often return home with the scent of Adorabelle on her hand and, stroking White Chin, she would happily describe to him all the events of her day. White Chin understood from these smells that Kirstie too was keeping her own tabs on the long-haired cat. However, he missed the truth of it, being that Kirstie enjoyed Kay's friendship and gossip, and playing with Adorabelle was only one of several attractions for her. He also missed the significance of Kirstie telling him excitedly about Adorabelle getting fat 'and what, White Chin, do you make of that?'

The farm, and the movements of animals and people around it, was of great interest to the little cat and he spent the majority of his time within its boundaries. He was especially curious about what it was that John and Shep did on the quad bike. Shep knew of course, but being a dog, he kept it to himself. One morning when White Chin was in the yard, he heard the bike and trailer going up into the next field, so he trotted off across the yard, squeezed under the fence and stood at the edge of the grass watching.

Sheep were still gathered by the gate where John had poured their treacle into the round wheel lick-feeder. They were busy fighting over it, getting their front feet right into the feeder with the treacle so they looked as if they were wearing sticky brown bibs. John, who was across the field, stopped the bike and released his cargo of lambs and mothers. The ewes were glad to have their freedom and quickly scampered towards the beloved treacle. The lambs being new to all this turned as a group towards White Chin and stared at him in a worried way, but he maintained a tactful distance, until they too ran off after their hungry mothers. As John set off again and opened the next gate a tide of sheep surged after him, milling around him and his bike, blathering loudly.

White Chin followed, attracted by the cries of the sheep, which were more passionate than he had heard before. John drove his quad bike on through the sheep with Shep riding pillion, heading for the next lick-feeder, and the sheep stampeded after him. He stopped the bike and started to carry the large container of treacle ready for pouring, but a particularly greedy ewe at the head of the stampede pushed into him with her full weight. The farmer crashed forward on his face, falling on top of the container full of treacle, which split and started to ooze its gooey contents all over him, and on the ground nearby. Immediately the rest of the flock clambered over him and on him and around him to get at the delicious sugary treat. The noise of triumphant sheep was deafening.

Shep stood close by watching his master anxiously, awaiting orders, uncertain what to do. When John finally levered himself up from the heaving mountain of sheep above him, Shep didn't recognize the words that the farmer said as being any order that he could follow. The sheep however seemed content enough.

White Chin turned back to the farm thoughtfully. So that was what John and Shep did on the quad bike when they went out.

They played with the sheep.

## 19

## More deadly than the male

Kirstie returned to school and, with that, life around the farm became less interesting for the black-and-white cat. White Chin now started to call on Lake House more regularly. He enjoyed Adorabelle's company and, if he was patient enough, she more often than not would spend some time with him. They developed an understanding.

In recent days, however, it had been different. Adorabelle had stopped coming outside. White Chin felt sad all over again. He had been so careful with their friendship and it had felt trusting and good. He had, though, for some time, sensed a change in his beautiful long-haired friend. Her moods were strange and unpredictable and she smelt different. A deep animal instinct made him know that something was happening to Adorabelle, but he couldn't properly work it out. He was sure it was nothing to do with her missing leg. Wondering what it was all about, he trotted up into the courtyard of Lake House with an air of purpose about him, determined to find out.

White Chin scented the area around the house and its studio. People had come and gone recently, including Kirstie, but there was no recent trace of Adorabelle, so she hadn't been outside since his last visit. That must mean she was staying indoors for a reason – but what?

He had often inspected the house from the garden, but without scent or sound to guide him it was difficult to tell where inside the building Adorabelle might be. He sometimes heard Kay talking as she moved around the house, but it didn't mean she was talking to Adorabelle. She had a special way of speaking to her cat, which White Chin recognised, and he hoped he might hear that sound as a pointer, but he didn't.

At the back of the building there was a metal fire escape which led up to a balcony outside the bathroom. Risking the shrieks of abuse he might receive from Adorabelle's owner he set off up the ladder. It was surprisingly easy to ascend and when he got to the balcony he was able to peer through the windows. Nothing. There were thin white curtains in the way and he could barely see anything. Now the problem was how to get back down. Backwards seemed the only way. It was very awkward and White Chin's feet kept slipping from the steps of the ladder. Half-way down he gave up and shuffling his backend through the ladder, he faced outwards and jumped to the ground making a great thump as he landed. He sat back and looked up at the house, sure she was in there.

He walked around to the front door and looked up at the window. This was the same window from which that woman had thrown water at him all those weeks ago. Adorabelle might be up in that room, he guessed. There wasn't any way that he could reach the window from where he stood now. He followed the wall around to the gable end and looked up at the window there. There was an ancient wisteria leaning against the wall and it passed close to one side of the window. He would be able to climb the gnarled main trunk and look in that way. White Chin started his ascent and the going was good. He soon found himself on the windowsill protected by the dense foliage and heady purple fronds of the tree. Sitting still, he waited for his eyes to adjust to the darker interior.

He was looking into a long gallery bedroom. Down in the corner, just below the windowsill, lay a large box. In the box, amid a load of clean, white bedding, he could see Adorabelle's back curled around. He watched for a long time.

She was busy, doing something, but he couldn't see what. He stayed very still as it was vital she didn't know he was there. He watched with the same deep concentration he would use when hunting. At last his patience was rewarded. Adorabelle rose and walked across the room towards some bowls of food at the far end. White Chin pulled back so she wouldn't see him if she turned, but he badly wanted to see what was in the big box on the floor she had been so busy with. The window was shut, but he could hear high-pitched wails through the glass. They were the cries of small animals!

White Chin tensed. He put his nose right up against the window, so that it steamed over a little as he peered through the glass. He could just make out the shape of two tiny black-and-white creatures like minute badgers, or enormous piebald mice or – surely not – kittens?

Their eyes were closed, their ears were halfway down the side of their heads and their mouths were open and red. They were making an extraordinary volume of noise. He listened, spellbound. It was infantile miaowing. These *were* kittens.

At that moment he saw a door open at the end of the room and Kay walked in, calling Adorabelle in her cutesy cat-voice. This held Adorabelle's attention at the far end of the room, giving White Chin a chance to get out of view. He climbed up to a higher branch of the wisteria which took him above and over to the right of the window so he couldn't be seen. But now he couldn't see either. He would wait.

He draped himself across a supporting branch like a small jungle cat hiding under an umbrella of leaves. There was the sound of the window being opened and suddenly Kay's voice seemed to come from somewhere terribly close, talking to Adorabelle. White Chin kept as still as a mouse and he heard the kittens stop wailing. Soon he heard Kay's footsteps as she walked out of the room and down the stairs, apparently still addressing Adorabelle, and everything went quiet.

Slowly White Chin inched his way down the tree to his look out post on the windowsill. He could see the two kittens wrapped around each other in a tight furry ball, apparently fast asleep. There was no sign of Adorabelle. White Chin sniffed the air and for the first time caught their scent. So this is what her behaviour had all been about!

The bedroom window was now open. The temptation was too great to resist. White Chin could just sneak in quickly and have a proper look at them. There was no sign of Adorabelle. He crept through the window, jumped gently down to the floor and walked stiffly towards the big box on the floor. As he neared the kittens they started to hiss at him, as, although blind, their sense of smell was powerful.

That was what did it. Chaos broke out!

White Chin was standing by the box, fascinated by the two tiny, defenceless, angry creatures hissing up at him, when, unknown to him, their mother re-entered the room and saw him standing there.

Adorabelle hurled herself across the room in a spitting, yowling frenzy of enraged fur and fury. White Chin didn't know what had hit him. He was absolutely terrified. Of all the skirmishes in which he had been involved in, this was the most scary. The female cat seemed out of her mind! White Chin ran back against the wall. He wanted to get to the open window but Adorabelle held him at bay, away from the kittens.

He hurled himself at the other window on which stood large pot plants that hurtled to the ground, breaking into smithereens. Again and again he smashed his body against the glass of the closed window trying to get away from the fury incarnate, as the wildly angry she-cat came at him.

Kay entered the room, and started to yell curses at him as she saw the chaos. White Chin then saw the possibility of an exit and, galloping towards the woman, he scrabbled between her legs, knocking her slightly to one side and half leapt, half rolled down the stairs.

He found the front door and burst his way out through the cat flap and on to freedom, around the lake wall and over the bridge in the direction of the farm without stopping, scared stiff that if he turned round he might see the terrifying spectre of Adorabelle on his tail. At last White Chin reached the sanctuary of his farmhouse, where he was able to rest and reflect upon the ordeal he just endured.

Had all that unspeakable aggression really been on behalf of those two tiny scraps of fur? All he'd done was just have a look!

# 20

# New life

Kirstie had been so upset when she discovered that she had missed the kittens' birth, that Kay had had to calm her down by telling her that she could come to Lake House for kitten-visiting whenever she wanted and had shown her where to find the spare key.

Kirstie first saw them the day after White Chin had made his dramatic entry into Adorabelle's domain and her immediate question, when finally setting her eyes upon the tiny kittens, was exactly who did Kay think the father might be? Kay groaned and then answered in a bored drawly sort of voice.

'Take a *really* good look at those two, honey, and tell me exactly who *you* think might have been their dad?

No clues now, but they're both black-and-white, although the white from their Mom seems to have won out. So okay just where *did* that black come from, do you think?' Kay laughed. She then bent down and stroked the two kittens under Adorabelle's chin. A powerful motherly pride glowed in the cat's eyes as Kay, in spite of her pretend-bored voice, clearly admired the new offspring.

Kirstie looked at the kittens wonderingly. 'You think White Chin is their Dad?'

Kay rolled her eyes dramatically, implying an exaggerated 'Yes'.

'But they don't look as much like him as you'd think they should . . .?' Kirstie said.

'No, cos a true tuxedo cat should be mostly black, with white fur on the jaw, mouth, chest and paws and White Chin really is just that. These two kitties, while I have no doubt they are his, are slightly different. Look . . .' and Kay bent down and picked up the female kitten. The kitten miaowed loudly, while her mother looked on with obvious concern, eyes large and watchful.

'This little one here is a perfect example of the "mask and mantle" pattern. Look, see, she seems to be wearing a black eye mask over her white face and supporting a black mantle along her back.'

'Ohhhh, that's so cute! Please let me hold her.' Kirstie took the wriggling kitten who was miaowing her protest ever more loudly, and held her on the palm of her hand. But the tiny blind kitten was so unhappy that Kirstie quickly placed her back into the tender care of her mother, who licked her with violent thoroughness to remove all human smells from her.

'So what about her brother?' Kirstie asked.

'Yup, he's a classic mask and mantle also, but his mask just slipped off that one eye, so it's a skewed one-eyed mask,' Kay grinned happily.

'So they're like teeny weeny Batmans. How sweet!' Kirstie tickled the boy kitten under his chin. He didn't like it much and hissed crossly at her. 'Whoops. Not really like little Batmans 'cos they've got white ears and white paws instead of black. Oh Kay, now you see how cute they are, you will keep them won't you? '

'I'll do no such thing! They'll be rehomed as soon as may be. If I'd had my way, Adorabelle would never have had them in the first place. She can mother them for however long it takes until they are weaned and then they'll have to go.'

Kirstie, shocked a little, pushed her lower lip out in silent protest.

Kay glanced at the young girl and added in a gentler voice, 'Adorabelle has gone through the mill, you know. It will do her good to just look after herself and I will take good care of my darling girl, you'll see. I'm a one-cat woman.'

As Kirstie watched Adorabelle tenderly licking her precious kittens on their clean white bed, she recalled the terrible day of the snaring accident and how frantic

White Chin had been, going back and forth, trying to rescue Adorabelle and not knowing what to do. Now, at last, she understood why it had mattered so much to him. She was his lady-love!

'Poor little White Chin,' she murmured, dreamily.

'Poor little White Chin be darned, first off fathering kittens left, right and centre and then on top of that breaking and entering! I've had quite enough of your cat for the moment, I'll tell you,' Kay retorted fiercely.

Kirstie was then treated to a fabulously dramatic retelling of the events that had taken place. Kay was still hopping mad at the assault that had been done to her plants and their containers, not to mention her house and her darling Adorabelle and Kirstie was spared nothing in the detail. Kirstie found it hard not to giggle at some of the outrageous things that White Chin was supposed to have done, while trying to flee the fury of Adorabelle. As Kirstie listened to Kay's version of events, even allowing that she was enjoying telling a good story, it did seem that the general mess and havoc that White Chin had left in his wake was a bit special!

Although Kay seemed to think it perfectly natural that Adorabelle had seen White Chin off in the way that she had, Kirstie didn't understand it and asked her why Adorabelle had gone so totally 'berserk' especially since White Chin was the father. Kay pulled a book off one of her bookshelves and pointed to a poem. It was called 'The Female of the Species' and it was by Rudyard Kipling. Kirstie read about the she-bear being in an instant a "white-hot, wild, wakened female of the species warring as for spouse and child" with "unprovoked and awful charges", which was what White Chin had been in receipt of – unprovoked and awful charges. Adorabelle's motherly instinct was more powerful than any other emotion in her being and she would protect her kittens against anyone and anything even if it meant fighting to the death.

After hearing at such length about White Chin's wrongdoings, Kirstie, fearful that Kay might go on to say further unfriendly things about her beloved tomcat, now changed the subject.

'What're you going to call the kittens?'

'I'm not going to name them, they're going to other homes. You can name them, if you like?'

Kirstie smiled and then pulled her brows together, thinking. At school this term they were doing *Alice*. She was playing one of the Alices, but that was a hopeless sort of cat name. On the other hand her two best friends Olivia and Lizzie were playing the Dodo and the Griffin.

'How 'bout Dodo for the girl kitten? No! Dodie's better. And Griffin for the boy?'

'Fine! Perfect! Sorted!'

And so Dodie and Griffin is what they became.

Kirstie watched the kittens' progress with fascination. For the first week Dodie and Griffin stayed by their mother, never moving from the box. On the few occasions when they were left on their own, while Adorabelle ate or briefly went out, they huddled together for their own warmth and never moved. Their eyes stayed firmly shut all week, but Kirstie, who sneaked in to see them nearly every day, straight after school, became spellbound by their progress. She was amused that every time she picked them up they still miaowed or hissed as if she was murdering them.

On the third Sunday after the kittens' birth Kirstie was thrilled by the sight that met her. In front of her the two kittens were sitting up, leaning against each other for support in a slightly uncertain way, like wobbly bookends.

Dodie, the little black female, had her head up above her brother Griffin and both of them were peeping through newly ungummed eyelids. As Kirstie looked down at them she could see the glistening pools of four milky blue eyes twinkling back at her. And as she bent down Griffin opened his mouth wide and gave a long strong hiss.

## 21

# And this is my friend

White Chin skulked around Old Bridge Farm, keeping well out of the way of Lake House and the frenzied Adorabelle. He wanted no more of the unpredictable she-cat for the moment, or those kittens, who seemed to be the real cause of all his problems. Life at the farm however had ceased to hold the same charms it had for him when Kirstie had been there all the time. Now White Chin saw little of her as she always came home late, smelling not just of Adorabelle, but of those troublesome kittens.

Added to that, there continued to be tension inside the farmhouse between him and Dilly. Her unrelenting stare made getting into Kirstie's bedroom at night something of a trial and sometimes White Chin just gave up the battle. Kirstie often fell asleep before realising he needed to be rescued!

During daylight hours he spent much of his time in the fields of the farmstead, hunting mice. A favourite haunt of his was the pasture where Buster was most often to be found. Having previously been wary of the pony, he now understood that Buster would never, knowingly, do him any harm. He was large, but he was gentle.

The cat got the impression that the pony was bored. Buster spent hours by the gate, waiting for something to happen. He would stand in the same spot, resting his hind leg, with his head down, his ears flopped in neutral, apparently on the edge of falling asleep. At other times he would spend long minutes on end pawing the ground and whinnying for no reason.

One day when White Chin went down to the pasture, he was startled to find Buster galloping around and around the outer limits of the field with his head facing the fence as he went, as if he was on a mission. White Chin squeezed under the gate, intending to sit down in a much-loved corner to start on a serious mouse hunt. This involved never taking his eyes off a tiny hole in the ground for however long it took, but the pony's relentless galloping distracted him. He crouched down in the grass, resting, and watched Buster do his mad circuits instead.

Suddenly it was all over. Buster slowed from a gallop

to a canter to a trot to a walk and finally he stood still and bent his head to crop the grass as if he had never been running like a crazy thing in the first place. He had just taken his third mouthful, when he stopped, and with spikes of now-forgotten grass still dangling from his mouth, he pricked his ears sharply forward, opened wide his nostrils and scented the air from where White Chin was crouched.

The cat tensed as the pony gazed at him with huge gentle brown eyes. The pony, now chewing slowly again, started to walk towards the little cat. There was a softness in his look and White Chin recognised the friendliness of his gaze. He stood as Buster got closer, but even so he felt very small. He looked up at the pony looming over him. Very gently the great horsey giant lowered his head and blew gently into White Chin's ear and then nibble-licked the fur on the little cat's back. White Chin loved the warmth and the gentleness of the caress and he gently headbutted Buster in return and rubbed the back of his ears against his huge soft nostrils.

From that moment on a strong bond developed between the little cat and the large pony. White Chin would regularly seek out Buster in stable or field, and the pony never failed to respond with gentle affection.

The biggest family get-together at Old Bridge Farm was always at the midday meals on Saturday and Sunday.

Being a busy farm other meals could be hit or miss, but Joan was very keen that they should spend time together as a family at least at the weekends, and update each other on their doings.

This Saturday it was five weeks since the kittens had been born over at Lake House. Kirstie couldn't stop chattering about their antics and how completely brilliant they were, when suddenly the wind was taken out of her sails by her mother asking her exactly when she thought she might next give poor Buster some exercise. And while on the subject of neglected animals, poor old White Chin didn't get much of a look-in either. Kirstie knew her Mum was right but she didn't like being reminded of it. It wasn't her fault after all, she just had so much on right now!

Feeling uncomfortable about the exchange that had just taken place she didn't dare tell them that Kay was getting so fed up with the kittens that she was going to throw them out. They needed a home and that had to be Kirstie's next project. It was too awful to even *begin* to think how she was going to tackle that problem.

Kirstie got up from the table and was just about to leave the room when her parents started talking about the lamping episode again. John suddenly cleared his throat like he did when he was going to make an announcement. He turned around and faced Kirstie and Alex.

'OK, now . . . listen you two, this is important! Doug is in touch with the Police Wildlife Officer for our area and they have been doing some investigations into both poaching episodes. The snares and the deer lamping. They seem to be taking it quite seriously.' He looked across at Joan and pulled a face. 'Although that piece that Kay thought she would plant in the *Gazette* hasn't helped matters.'

'Do they know who did it, then?' Alex asked enthusiastically.

'No, or not that they're telling me at any rate,' John replied. 'But the point is it's now official, and we need the police to get to the bottom of it.' John leaned forward and looked into the eyes of each of his children in turn. 'But the reason I am mentioning it to you now is that you're to stay out of it. You are not to talk of it at school or, Kirstie, when you are with Kay.'

Brother and sister both nodded their agreement to this request. Kirstie would be more than happy to avoid the subject with Kay for the rest of her life. It was the one thing that always made her feel really awkward whenever Kay mentioned it. So now, determined to have only the most positive of conversations with Kay when she next saw her, Kirstie paid more attention to Buster, hoping this might soften her parents up.

The next day, Sunday, Kirstie, good to her new resolution, tacked her pony up. He nuzzled her affectionately, excited at the unexpected attention. She paused and put her arms round his neck, inhaling his wonderful horsey smell.

'Oh, Buster, you smell so good I could eat you. I do

love you so much, you old thing. I do want to be with you more, honestly. It's just finding the time to do EVERYTHING, that's the trouble.'

Kirstie tacked him up and the two of them trotted off through the woods the full breadth of Troonholme Park. Kirstie, yet again, saw no obvious sign of where the new snare might have been placed, but she was careful not to stray off the main path at any point. It would be too horrible to imagine if Buster got trapped in the snare. She walked Buster back into the courtyard of Lake House and tied him to the gate.

As Kirstie reached the door, Kay met her on her way out, but as she dashed for her car she muttered to Kirstie that the Police Wildlife Officer had called yesterday, and didn't seem over-impressed with her evidence against Doug, as it had appeared in the *Gazette* the other month.

'Who cares?' she laughed. 'It will have made Doug think twice about some of the things he *does* do!' And without waiting for a response from the horrified Kirstie, she folded herself into her red sports car, banged the door shut and rattled off past the patient Buster in a flurry of exhaust and expensive scent.

Kirstie, who came and went in this house as she pleased, now settled down for a play session with the kittens, although with Buster tied up outside she had to keep it short. It was worth it, though, as every minute spent with the kittens now was a glorious entertainment.

It was a sad fact, Kirstie realised however, that

whenever you left them you found you had raw red scratch marks on the backs of your hands and all up your legs. People knew where you'd been! Their claws were like tiny needles and seemed to be sticking out all the time to help them in every movement. Clothes made irresistible climbing frames. As Kirstie gazed adoringly at the kittens she realised that they were now much prettier than they had been when they were first born. Their ears were pert and up at the top of their heads and their baby fluff was thick and fuzzy – they looked as if their fur was going to have the luxurious Maine Coone length to it. Their eyes too had changed and were now widely open, focussed and the blue of periwinkles. Their heads seemed almost too big for their bodies, which finished in tiny sticking-out little tails. She scooped them up, wriggling, into her arms and crooned gently:

'Pussy cat, pussy cat, wilt thou be mine?
Thou shalt not wash dishes, nor feed yet the swine,
But sit on a cushion and sew a fine seam
And feed upon strawberries, sugar and cream.'

Oh how she longed to take them home with her.

## 22

# Double, double, toil and trouble

One day, as Kirstie left Old Bridge Farm to cycle up to the kittens, White Chin, who had been watching for just such a chance, followed her along the country road and over the bridge towards Lake House. He kept to the hedgerows and he fell some distance behind her.

When Kirstie got to the front door she rang the doorbell and walked in as usual. When the little cat reached the house a few minutes later, he saw her bike against the wall, and sniffed the forecourt. She had arrived all right, and not that long ago!

White Chin knew from the smell around Lake House and the scent of the kittens on Kirstie's hands and clothes, that she came here. Often. He wanted to see for himself what went on.

He considered using the cat flap and rejected it. It had bad memories for him. He sidled around to the gable-end window and climbed the wisteria. The bedroom window was slightly open at the top but not enough to allow him in. White Chin watched. He could see Kirstie bent over what looked like a big group of cats by the far wall, judging by all the fur and the fluffy tail ends that were just visible. She seemed to be playing with them and talking to them. He felt an ache of sadness and lowered his head. He looked away, deep in thought. His attention was drawn again to the room by hearing voices through the glass and he turned back to watch. Kirstie had moved away from the cats and was now perched on the edge of the bed, facing, from the sound of her, Kay, who was sitting out of his sight somewhere talking long and loudly.

Now that Kirstie had moved, White Chin could see them! Across the room lying on the floor with her back to the wall was Adorabelle and she had her front leg over the girl kitten, Dodie, whom she was grooming. Next to her, lying on the floor behind Dodie, was Griffin. The kittens looked huge to White Chin. In fact they were only eight weeks old, but their fur had grown long and fluffy, and although they had his colouring, they had the distinctive look of their Maine Coone mother. At that moment both the kittens seemed to catch his scent, or hear him and put their heads up to look straight through the window at him. Without pausing for breath White Chin retreated down the wisteria tree. He was in no mood for a three-cat attack.

Kirstie was well aware that Griffin and Dodie were continuing to drive Kay crazy as they became ever more active. They delighted in their new-found skills of climbing, chewing, biting and play-fighting which they did for longer each day, creating ever more destructive messes in their wake. They also had a way of falling asleep wherever they found themselves, so they were constantly getting locked into rooms and cupboards.

Adorabelle left them on their own for a little longer each day. Now, at eight weeks old, she still allowed them to suckle her milk occasionally, but very soon she would stop that. They had been eating solids for some time and they were left by their mother to make use of their litter tray and groom themselves on their own, which in the main they did, although not always.

Kay, never one to hold back on relaying the dramatic events in her life, gave Kirstie a graphic account of the kittens' latest wrongdoings. The catalogue ran as follows:

1. The wrecking of a pair of Prada trousers – Dodie and Griffin as a pair;

2. Disappearing for hours and then being found amid the potato peelings inside the swing bin containing

the kitchen waste – Griffin;

3. Systematically eating the cat litter granules and then being very sick – Dodie;

4. Accidents too numerous to count, outside the cat litter tray – Griffin;

5. Going to sleep on clean clothes inside the drying machine and doing three sick-making circuits before being rescued by Kay who thought at first that she was a black-and-white fleece.

Altogether the pair of them were being very naughty and tiresome. These outrages, and the way Kay told them, made Kirstie laugh, but Kay's next statement made her heart miss a beat.

Kay announced that she'd had enough. This was it. She'd reached the end of the road. The kittens would have to go within the week. She said she would advertise in the local paper, but if all else failed she would take them to the pet shop. Kirstie wailed out in horror. She knew already, from having heard the big man when he was dumping White Chin, what awful things could happen to kittens sold from pet shops. She had to stop this, but how?

Kirstie returned to Old Bridge Farm in a state of high agitation. She knew she didn't have much time to find the kittens another, *safe* home. She had hoped she would have more time to work on her parents. She begged and pleaded, but immediately encountered fierce opposition from both Mum and Dad, although her Mum was the worst.

'Kirstie, you take on more than you should, as it is. You desperately wanted White Chin here and when your Dad brought him home when he was wounded you promised you would look after him. Now, instead, you seem to be spending all your time on that play of yours. And if you're not on with that, you're sending silly messages to your friend Olivia or talking to her for hours on the phone. And these days it seems to be all Lake House and kittens. Buster and White Chin never get a look in.'

It went on and on with Kirstie throwing in the odd 'unfair', which was immediately countered by another protest from Joan. John put his head down and went quiet. Eventually, however, following an especially powerful plea by Kirstie, who was shameless in the way she worked on her father, it was agreed that the pair of kittens would be allowed to come to Old Bridge Farm on a temporary basis.

'But, young woman, only until more suitable arrangements can be found,' her Mum added in what she probably thought was a firm voice.

Kirstie was thrilled. It had been very hard-won but now she would now have all the animals she loved under one roof! Her roof! Well, almost. Buster's stable was attached to the house, so it sort of counted as one roof! When the summer holidays started she'd have loads of time for them all.

All was peaceful within the farmhouse. Stubs was outside in the cow shed, minding his own business, which at this particular moment involved lying in a manger snoozing. Shep was out with John playing with sheep. Dilly was skulking near the hen coops waiting for Joan to put out their feed, and White Chin was out in the pasture with Buster, playing the game of dare that he so enjoyed, walking between Buster's hooves as he grazed.

White Chin looked up as he heard the Land Rover rattle over the cattle grid into the yard. He had seen Kirstie get into it earlier with Joan, so he wandered slowly towards the farmhouse to see if a treat or a cuddle might be in the offing. They were busy unloading all sorts of weird things. A platform with ropes round it, and a soft squashy thing that looked like a cat bed. They didn't seem to have much time for him, so he sauntered across the yard in the direction of Stubs who was sitting on the wall, watching.

That was when White Chin heard an unmistakable series of sounds that made him go rigid. He knew those voices! They were kitten mews of protest and complaint. He looked up and saw Stubs yawning, but behind the yawn he saw a glimmer of interest in the old cat's eye. White Chin let out a tiny mew of his own in spite of himself and, horror-struck, he walked slowly towards the farmhouse and the source of the sound.

Kirstie had just released the kittens into the kitchen. Griffin was nervous and cowered down at first, but Dodie sprang out with a miaow of satisfaction that she was at last released from her cruel captivity. Within seconds she and, shortly after, her brother started running round investigating everything. The smells were new and different from those where they had been born.

Although the kittens acted as if they were unaware of him, the same was not true of White Chin, who was frozen to the spot by the door. As the kittens became more adventurous in their investigations they came close to White Chin. Then they saw him and stopped. He stared at them with his back hunched, showing them large eyes. Unable to stop himself he hissed in irritation at their invasion. As his anger increased, his hiss became a deep menacing growl. He then became fearful that Adorabelle, the furry fury, might come charging in any minute to defend her young.

Kirstie, who had been giggling at the proceedings, went across to White Chin and stroked him. Slowly his growl subsided and he licked his nose, doubtfully. Dodie and Griffin stared back at him, unsure what to make of him. He was the first angry feline they had seen. He lowered himself down on his belly and turned his ears in a flattened out position. He hissed a bit and licked his nose in between.

Kirstie laughed as she watched them, then said, 'Mum, I think he's actually frightened. That's crazy. They're only babies.'

'I know, but they're new and on his territory, so it's a threat for him,' she answered, distractedly. 'And just wait until Dilly sees them!'

Sure enough, when Dilly did come into the kitchen a little later, everything unfurled into uproar. Dilly spat at the kittens, then she turned and hissed at White Chin, who looked most put out by this further insult and growled back fiercely. The kittens were frightened by these sounds of open aggression and did baby hisses in stereo, which made Dilly growl more loudly.

Dilly's growl had an electric effect on the kittens, who ran straight up the long curtains by the window. Halfway up, they lost their nerve and started mewling for help. The longer they clung to the curtains the louder came their cries. Joan, who had grabbed both Dilly and White Chin by the backs of their necks, shouted to Kirstie above the caterwauling to go and rescue the kittens from where they were dangling.

Kirstie had a terrible time trying to get the tiny claws of the frightened kittens unhooked from the fabric of the curtains, but finally she hauled them down to ground level again. While all this was going on White Chin and Dilly, a most unlikely couple if ever there was one, were half thrown out of the front door into the yard as if they were one cat with eight legs. There they quickly scuttled off in different directions, to seek the comfort of their favourite haunts in the blissfully kitten-free world of outside. Dodie and Griffin were left, for the remainder of the day, to continue their investigations of the farmhouse kitchen on their peaceful own.

White Chin sought out Stubs and the two touched noses, in sympathy. He would never become a real friend of Stubs, who was far too much of a loner to form any relationship with another cat, but from this time on there was an understanding between the two toms.

Life continued to be disrupted within the farmhouse, with regular bouts of hissing and spitting from both White Chin and Dilly as the kittens merrily took over – everything! The constant hissings became less frequent, but no stage was reached when either Dilly or White Chin were really comfortable in the presence of the kittens.

One day, Kirstie's two best friends Lizzie and Olivia came over. White Chin was there to greet them, but Olivia just ignored him and went straight over to the kittens, although Lizzie gave him a stroke as she passed. She smelt of dog so White Chin backed off and jumped on the windowsill. As he turned back to face the room he saw the three friends together, everything else forgotten. They all lay in a heap on the floor playing with the kittens, giggling and squawking when they got scratched.

White Chin turned away and thought his own thoughts.

## 23

# The pain in "spain"

The kittens provided Kirstie with endless fun. She found their playfulness impossible to resist. They were always getting up to and into things and often they got into trouble just as they had at Kay's, but life in the farmhouse was much more relaxed so their naughty doings were less disturbing to the farming family than they had been to the tempestuous artist. Even Alex, grudgingly, found them funny, although he complained that his scratched arms and legs were something he wouldn't have to put up with from his rabbit kits.

Kirstie's Mum had spoken to Kay on the phone. She'd said that she had taken Adorabelle to be neutered, and although recovering well from her operation, she seemed to be missing the kittens quite badly. Kay had added that the same was not true for her. She was happy to announce that she didn't miss the kittens one jot, although, she had added in an unusually quiet voice, she couldn't fail to notice that Kirstie had disappeared totally along with the kittens! When her Mum had relayed this to Kirstie, Kirstie had giggled at first on the kitten front. But when Joan suggested perhaps it was a bit hurtful to just dump people, rather as she had dumped her animals, Kirstie threw her Mum a guilty glance.

That weekend the whole family was involved in the annual labour of clipping the sheep and each of them had their allotted task. Kirstie's was to roll and tie the fleeces as they fell from her father's clippers. After an hour's work, her Dad stood up, massaging his sore back from bending over numerous sheep and swigged thirstily from his mug of tea. Her Mum and Alex had gone to gather in a further group of reluctant ewes and so there was a brief lull in the proceedings. Kirstie sat up on the fleece bench, swinging her legs, sucking at a long strand of hair thoughtfully. She had been thinking about not seeing Kay and was feeling a bit uncomfortable about it. When she started to talk, however, she opened with her favourite topic – kittens!

'They don't seem to miss Adorabelle anything like as much as she misses them. Do you think they *are* missing her?' Kirstie said to her Dad.

'If you are talking about those two little blighters

back in the kitchen I'm sure they are a bit. But I rather think that it's easier for the young ones. They're full of curiosity and life goes on. In fact, it gets more exciting. Whereas for the mother animal everything in her instinct is geared to make sure she's a good parent, which means that she's almost programmed to miss her young when they're taken away from her. But Adorabelle will be all right, don't worry. You've seen how sheep suffer for the first two or three days when their lambs are taken away, but they soon get back to grazing again, and regain the weight they lost when they were going through the missing-my-baby bit.'

'I know, I hate that – when the sheep call out all night long, wanting their lambs back. I think it's the saddest sound in the whole world. What's that horrid word for it?'

'It's called spaining, and we'll be starting with it in just over a month,' John said, tidying his mug out of the way before the next lot of sheep stampeded into the shed.

'But what does that silly word "spain" mean?' Kirstie asked.

'Oh it's one of those words farmers, well sheep farmers at any rate, have always used. It's a word my Dad used to say, and his Dad before him. To "spain" means to separate the lambs from their ewes, so they can be fully weaned. You know, when you need to start fattening the lambs for market, or if you are going to sell them on for breeding. It's a very old word.' As her father finished his explanation Kirstie sighed deeply and stuck out her bottom lip.

'I don't like it. It's a cruel word.'

Her father grinned sympathetically. At that point the shed doors opened to allow a further arrival of panting, baaing ewes and their adolescent offspring.

'I don't think it's the word, I think it's what it describes you don't like,' he shouted above the racket. She grinned and nodded and they started back on their shepherding labours.

That evening Kirstie cycled over to Lake House to see Kay and Adorabelle. Kay was warm in her welcome of her young friend and Kirstie felt doubly guilty for having stayed away for so long. Adorabelle was still confined to the house and, according to Kay, she seemed pretty out of sorts. Kay thought some of it might be a hangover from her anaesthetic and the discomfort of her surgery but mainly, she reckoned, it was caused by the absence of her kittens.

When Dodie and Griffin were very small Kirstie had brought over a soft pink toy kitten as a plaything for them and it had remained behind when she took them away to Old Bridge Farm. At one point, when Adorabelle had been crying for her kittens, Kay had put the toy near her to keep her warm, but later the same day she was somewhat disturbed by the spectacle of her three-legged cat walking around the house holding the toy in her mouth for minutes on end, repeatedly calling for her young.

Kirstie stroked Adorabelle, and looked deep into her large shining eyes.

'Don't be sad, Adorabelle. Your lovely kittens are all right, honestly. Trust me.'

The beautiful Maine Coone cat lay in a proud lion-like position; but next to her, where her missing leg should be, lay the soft pink kitten-toy.

## 24

## I was adored once too

White Chin spent more and more time outside keeping himself to himself. When he had originally spied the kittens through the window at Lake House he had been interested in who they were and what they were about. At that time he was eager to know more. But now they were here, on his home patch, he felt very differently.

Their unending appetite for play was infuriating and it made being inside the farmhouse disagreeable. It never stopped. Their demands were endless. All the time he found himself having to watch out for his tail. They would pounce – how they would pounce! And the pain from those teeth and claws! All movement inside the house had to be made in the full expectation of a savage ambush any minute. Sometimes White Chin would instinctively spring up and around, like some mad thing, just to make sure they weren't there, right behind him. Each piece of furniture now became a threat, providing cover for ambushing kittens and giving them the power of stealth. *They* thought it was funny, but it wasn't. It was terrible!

When inside, White Chin and Dilly kept a truce with each other in the face of the kitten offensive, and both of them chose their times for being inside with care. In spite of the domestic ceasefire, however, White Chin avoided Dilly when out on the farm, as her manners there left much to be desired. Being stared at was considerably more threatening than being nagged by the kittens to play and it seemed to White Chin that Dilly was taking out her anger at the kitten-invasion by stalking him when they were outside. She had never before been on his back with quite this amount of ill will.

White Chin became nervous and withdrawn and he began to walk around the place with his eyes staring wide, ready to run from anything and everything. Added to this, as he watched Kirstie playing endlessly with the kittens he longed for her to turn her attention to him. He became very sad.

His one remaining pleasure was his night-time snuggle with the young girl and he made it his business to be around at the right moment so that Kirstie wouldn't fail to take him up with her. He was aware, too, that Dilly was extra vigilant in keeping watch over

Joan from the landing sofa as usual. Joan was the only being the Bengal cat really trusted. The kittens continued to sleep downstairs, completely unaware of the ripples of distress they had caused.

Gramps came to stay. It had been many months since he had been persuaded to visit and Kirstie in particular was longing for him to meet White Chin and of course, now, the kittens. Joan's excuse for uprooting her Dad had been so that he might see Kirstie's performance as one of the six Alices in her end-of-term school musical the following night.

His visit started badly. He was tired and grumpy when he arrived and as soon as he had settled down in the armchair the kittens had climbed up him, as they did to anyone who sat still long enough. For Gramps it was a first and they shot up his thin bony legs, scratching him badly even through his trousers, so he bled making his trousers all messy. He then trod on Dodie by accident as he levered himself out of his chair and she made a terrible fuss as if he had really damaged her. She kept crying for ages, which agitated Kirstie and made Gramps even crosser. He started mumbling in a corner about getting home now, while he was still in one piece.

It went from bad to worse. Griffin went missing. He couldn't be found anywhere. To begin with it was a bit of a laugh, but soon the whole household was disrupted while search parties went in pursuit of him. Dodie, who had recovered from being trampled on, seemed calm and then, in all the confusion, she also disappeared. Kirstie trailed from room to room, looking for the kittens in a slightly distracted way, while chanting out songs from the musical, so everyone was treated to endless repeats of:

'I wish I hadn't cried so much, I wish I hadn't cried so much, I'm shrinking and I'm growing, I'm coming and I'm going, I'm tired of never knowing who I am.'

Eventually Gramps got out of his chair groaning and said, 'Wish I could be going at this rate.' But although everyone else laughed, Kirstie didn't find it funny.

Kirstie was in the kitchen when Dodie appeared as if from nowhere, and sat down in front of the washing machine. The kitten had a knowing air about her.

'Dodie, what are you doing here and where's Griffin gone?' Kirstie asked in a normal non-Alice sort of voice. The kitten leant forward and tried to push her paw through the minute crack between the washing machine and the other cupboard in the corner. Gramps, who was, by this time, clutching a restoring glass of wine, came into the utility room and looked thoughtfully at the kitten over Kirstie's shoulder.

'I think that little blighter is trying to tell you something, Kirstie-girl,' he said.

The kitten continued to sit staring at the machine. Gramps shuffled off towards the box where all the tools were kept and came back with a torch. Dodie moved to one side quickly in case Gramps trod on her again. The old man shone the torch down the narrow crack.

'Ha, just as I thought! So what the heck do you think you're doing there, young fellow?'

Kirstie eagerly grabbed the flashlight from her Granddad and peering down the dark crack she saw the glow of a pair of cat's eyes reflecting back at her. As she moved the torch up and down she could just make out the outline of a head and pair of ears festooned with strands of cobwebs.

After a huge kerfuffle which involved the washing machine being unplumbed so that it could be hauled out of its corner where it was lodged at an angle, they finally persuaded a very relaxed Griffin to come out of his dank dusty corner. It seemed he had crawled down an opening under the sink and behind the units until he had reached the point of no return, where he could see his sister staring at him through the crack. Having regained his freedom, he looked mightily pleased with himself, as he sauntered across to his food bowl. Gramps announced in a flat voice that he remained unimpressed by the kittens and their doings.

Later that evening the old man entertained the household with accounts of his close neighbour, Enid Batty, who clearly provided him with much merriment. His house was quite remote and she lived in the neighbouring homestead with all her animals. She was totally animal mad it seemed, as long as the creatures in question were female. Gramps explained with much relish that Enid claimed 'girls' were far more useful than their male counterparts, providing as they did such delicious offerings as milk and eggs and if you needed more females as they died out, you just borrowed a male of the species on a temporary basis. Gramps seemed to think this was very funny and fondly referred to Enid as 'Batty by name; batty by nature.'

As Gramps sat forward laughing in the big armchair under the tall lamp, his silver hair gleamed in the light and his moustache ends danced with a life of their own. Kirstie watched him fondly. He reminded her of a favourite wizard. The old man continued, with a deep chuckle, 'She actually bid for – and won – two fertile goose eggs in an eBay auction because one of her geese had gone broody. She calls them all names from characters in Beatrix Potter stories. And I suppose as far as the animals are concerned that's fair enough.' He sat back and took a sip from his glass. 'But it doesn't stop there. She gives names to other things around the place too. Take her motorbike for example. It's called Jeremy Fisher for heaven's sake and she calls the sidecar Mrs Fisher.'

'Why's the motorbike male? I thought vehicles were always female?' Joan asked laughing.

'Yup, I asked her that too. She just put her hands on her hips and said: "Honestly, Dr Parfitt, think about it! How could something so hefty and grunty and smelly be a she?" To which, frankly, there was no polite reply that I could easily think of.'

White Chin, who had been sitting near Gramps as he talked, really wanted to get closer to him. Something drew him towards the old man and he jumped up onto the arm of the chair and slowly, gently, crept onto his knee where, sitting down, he purred quietly to himself letting his head drop as he relaxed more deeply. As the old man talked his hand went down to White Chin's head, where it gently stroked behind the cat's ears. The purring became deeper and steadier. Gramps grinned.

'I must say, this cat here is rather charming. He seems to like me. I don't think much to cats as a general rule, but this one's a bit of all right.' he said. Kirstie was thrilled when she heard Gramps say this, and as he looked down at the cat on his knee, she put both thumbs up to her mother.

The rest of the evening passed more or less peacefully, with the kittens only making one half-hearted attempt to harass White Chin. Gramps shushed them off very quickly to make absolutely sure they didn't attack his legs again. The older cat remained curled up on the old man's knee out of harm's way for quite some time. That is until Dilly came in and started staring, at which point White Chin hissed at her and withdrew to sit on a chair under the table until it was time to go upstairs.

The long-awaited performance of Kirstie's school production of *Alice, the Musical* the following night was more successful than Kirstie had dared to dream –

she didn't forget her words once. After they had all returned to the farmhouse and eaten a late meal, and in the relaxed mood following a job well done, Kirstie dropped the small bombshell she'd been holding back until the play was out of the way.

Olivia had invited her to stay for several weeks of the holidays. The plan was that her father would come over, box Buster up and take him over with the girls, so they could go out riding together around the area where Olivia lived. Kirstie had been longing to do this, as sometimes riding out on her own could feel lonesome.

After much discussion, and several phone calls to Olivia's parents and following some powerful persuasion on her behalf by Gramps, who could never bear to see his beloved granddaughter denied anything, John and Joan finally agreed that Kirstie could go.

After Gramps left, everyone in the farmhouse seemed to have his or her mind somewhere else and White Chin felt quite out of things. Something must be about to happen? Kirstie in particular seemed to be in a world of her own and although he still slept in her room at night, White Chin sensed that his young human friend's mind was elsewhere.

Feeling abandoned, White Chin more often than not sought the company of Buster. Their communication was limited but their trust and liking of each other was deep. Buster on hearing or smelling White Chin would drop his head to the ground and snuffle the little cat in greeting, and White Chin had now discovered that if he jumped up onto the gatepost he could butt Buster's great big long face with the side of his head. He did this very gently because Buster always took such pains to be gentle with him. When he rubbed his head against Buster, the pony would sigh sweetly through his velvety nose.

One day an unknown Land Rover with a trailer turned up, driven by Olivia's Dad and White Chin went into the yard to watch. Kirstie was standing in the yard waiting, and as it drove in she jumped up and down excitedly. The Land Rover did a neat turn and Olivia's grinning face could be seen through the windscreen. With a flurry of long brown hair and a flash of smart cream jodhpurs Olivia jumped down and flashed a shy smile at the assembled company. With some mild expletives the ramp was lowered and the loading of Buster started. The game little Fell pony looked across at White Chin with a surprised expression on his face, but as Kirstie led him up into the narrow compartment he did all that was asked of him.

So, with lots of banging and shouting and gales of laughter, all was ready and the Land Rover and trailer kitted up with its cargo was prepared to set off. Because of all the noise White Chin had retired inside the farmhouse. This seemed no place for him! Kirstie had hugged her parents farewell and had climbed in next to

Olivia when she suddenly remembered she hadn't said goodbye to the kittens or to White Chin.

'Stop, stop. Sorry, sorry. Gotta say goodbye to the furries. Won't be a tick, promise.' And she jumped out again and rushed across the yard. She ran into the house and picked up Griffin and Dodie and told them to be good and then charged around looking for White Chin. She couldn't find him anywhere so since she was being called she yelled a goodbye into the air and ran outside. The Land Rover and trailer rumbled over the cattle grid bearing away the two school friends and Buster into the wild blue yonder.

White Chin had gone up to Kirstie's bedroom to escape the hubbub and to make sure he avoided the kittens. As he heard the engine of the Land Rover he jumped onto the windowsill and looked out. He caught a glimpse of Buster's head twisting around in a questioning way as the trailer paused at the cattle grid, and then, as it rattled off, the last sight he had was of the pony swaying gently from side to side. White Chin watched until he could see them no more. He knew that Kirstie would come back very soon. She always did. He would wait for her.

## 25

## Waving his wild tail

White Chin felt more lonely than he could ever remember being. Kirstie didn't come back very soon after all! Joan and John both talked to him and fed him, and so did Alex, sometimes, but it wasn't the same with any of them. Kirstie had been his special champion, always. White Chin now realised that Kirstie had protected him more than he had understood. Protected him from Dilly, from the kittens, from the world!

And at night, so much then, he missed her company. The cuddles, the talk, the strokes, the warmth. He knew which crook of her leg to lie in. Which side she slept on most. He knew the rhythm of her breathing and when she might turn over and knock him off the bed. When she might fling her arm out and how he could get her to stroke him even in her sleep by nestling against her. When he had been alone in the woods, although sometimes he had been frightened, cold and hungry he had been able to cope. The loneliness he felt here was different. Kirstie was the centre of his world and she had gone. And not only that, but his friend Buster had gone too. White Chin, in the way of cats, understood that Buster wasn't there, but he continued to go up to the pasture just to check and would often sit on Buster's empty stable door, just waiting.

The friction from Dilly was increasing, and the long nights inside the farmhouse were becoming a real trial for him. These days White Chin no longer knew where he could sleep without being harassed. The aggression came mainly from Dilly's stares, but sometimes it went further than that. For no good reason that White Chin could see he would suddenly be in receipt of full frontal attacks when she would claw out fistfuls of his fur, or chase him up the stairs and rip out his fur from behind. He never fought back against her, being the gentle and mannerly cat he was.

Now, to the horror of all three cats and sometimes even Shep, the kittens were allowed the freedom of the farm. They had had their second lot of injections and Joan was glad to be relieved of having to clean a litter tray daily, so now they came and went at will. They often got into trouble and Joan and John found themselves involved at least once a day in Operation Kitten Rescue!

White Chin spent more time hunting, as he had in the old days. One morning, instead of stalking Buster's field for rodents and rabbits, he walked the other way, over the bridge to Lake House. He approached with caution. He was unsure what he would find, although at least there would be no kittens there!

As he walked slowly along by the lake wall he caught sight of Adorabelle's white coat gleaming in the sunshine and her dark bushy tail twitching slightly. She was stretched out majestically, sunbathing. He had already scented her on the air and knew she was close by. He miaowed a nearly silent greeting to her. She slowly rose, yawned widely and stretched herself, then turned and walked towards him. He gently headbutted her and she butted him back and they touched noses. They both sat down and on and off watched each other. They walked and ran and played together briefly and then stopped. When they sat down again, Adorabelle gently licked White Chin around his head and his ears and his eyes. He closed his eyes and purred deeply in pleasure. They moved apart but stayed lying within sight of each other in a companionably close apartness.

Their friendship lived on, in spite of all that had happened to Adorabelle. She was recovered from the loss of her kittens and no longer needed the comfort of the pink toy. White Chin visited regularly and if Adorabelle felt in the right frame of mind they would spend time together playing. Sometimes, now, to escape the joint ordeals of the kittens and Dilly, White Chin took to sleeping again in the Lake House shed. But after a few days he would return to Old Bridge Farm. He needed to know if Kirstie and Buster had come back.

After a couple of nights at Lake House, White Chin returned to the farm in better spirits than he had experienced for some days. But Griffin and Dodie had other plans. They were waiting in ambush for him. As White Chin walked past the boundary fence into the yard, Griffin sprang on him from the wall above and landed squarely on his back, with his claws extended. His mouth was wide open and he was miaowing in fun, but White Chin, made angry by the assault, swung around to snarl fiercely at the kitten. The young animal crouched submissively but White Chin swatted him, hard, several times with his front foot. The kitten jumped back in surprised alarm and sought the comfort of his sister. They were silenced by what they had just seen.

It was no better inside the farmhouse. On White Chin's return Dilly became increasingly quarrelsome. Her pitiless staring was so threatening that without knowing why he did it, he found himself spraying the books in the bookcase on the landing where Dilly kept watch. She made a loud wailing noise announcing his evil doing to the world. The bedroom door opened and Joan came out as he made his final desperate flourish.

She was furious and shouted at him loudly. She picked him up, shaking him crossly, and carried him downstairs where she half threw him and half pushed him out of the front door. As he was ejected he heard Dilly's basso miaow.

Weeks passed and life on the farm became even more disagreeable. None of the other animals or any of the people seemed to have time for White Chin, or to care for him. He missed Kirstie and he couldn't understand why she'd gone away and left him. Nothing was the same any more. When he didn't sleep down at Lake House he now slept in the barn, but even that didn't work out. One night he and Stubs had a quarrel and a hissing dispute turned into a minor scrap, which made him feel even more at odds with all the creatures around him. Now he could no longer relax around the barn, let alone inside the house. He felt rootless and alone. What White Chin couldn't know was that all the time he was suffering, Joan was keeping a close eye on him.

The little cat spent more and more time now at Lake House and one night, after dark, when he was waiting to see if Adorabelle was going to come out – sometimes she did and sometimes she didn't – the cat Blue appeared. He hadn't seen Blue since the near fight they had had on the night when he wooed and won Adorabelle all those months ago. White Chin stared at Blue, but the other cat seemed to want to stay around. White Chin warned him off with a yowly sort of growl and Blue replied with a deep 'mneeoowwww' which sounded like he meant to hang about, all the same.

White Chin, although younger, was now the same weight and size as Blue and he was having none of this. Blue had been his sworn enemy for a long time. White Chin thrashed his tail violently against the ground. Blue bashed his up and down with equal force. The tension between the two cats increased and then Blue challenged White Chin, who slashed back with claws unsheathed. The cats rolled on the ground screaming and then fell apart as quickly as they had come together. The cat wails increased again and they moved towards each other, with their faces so close that they had nose pressed on nose and their eyes met in the middle. At this moment the lights went on and the bedroom window opened. White Chin should have realised what was going to happen, but he couldn't bear to give the advantage to Blue.

There was a loud sloshing sound and to their horror both cats were drenched with cold water, accompanied by shouts of, 'Shut up! Shut up! Shut up! How on earth can anyone get any sleep with that filthy noise going on? If you don't stop at once I will come down and put a hose on you and I'm not kidding!' With this rebuke the window was slammed shut and the lights went out. The dousing of water was surprisingly effective and both cats slunk off to their homes, unhappily wet and cold and with several cuts to be licked clean.

White Chin arrived home and, finding the downstairs window open, went inside the farmhouse to look for somewhere quiet and dry to clean his wounds. In Kirstie's empty bedroom, he found Griffin asleep on the bed. White Chin snarled crossly. Griffin got up and tried to play, but when White Chin would have none of it, Griffin wandered into the hallway and tried Dilly.

Dilly, however, got up and wandered across to the bookcase where there was still a residue of the smell from White Chin's spraying. The Bengal then turned about and sprayed the bookcase herself, after which she wailed out her special sneaky wail. Joan, on hearing this and knowing of old that it meant trouble, emerged from her room and saw and felt the warm wet patch along the books. She looked up and saw White Chin on Kirstie's bed and assumed he was the guilty party.

'Right, me lad. That's it. Enough's enough. Now it's out, out, out!' And out he went. That night and from then on, the house was out of bounds to him.

Joan went, as arranged, to see Kirstie at Olivia's house bearing clean clothes and horse fodder. Long serious talks were held on the subject of White Chin and Joan slowly explained that White Chin was deeply unhappy at the farm. He had become almost feral and when he was in the house, he looked utterly miserable. It was no kindness to keep him there. For his own good Joan would undertake to find him a new home.

As her mother talked, Kirstie became increasingly distressed. She knew well enough that she hadn't looked after him and had spent too much time playing with the kittens, but this was unbearable! She understood that he was unhappy but she was heartbroken that White Chin was to go away. It was only a little comfort when Joan told her that Gramps had said he would take White Chin 'on trial' with him and that Kirstie could come over to see him whenever she wished.

Joan tried to comfort her tear-stained daughter by explaining to her that White Chin in the end would be a much happier cat without all the other animals driving him mad. Joan explained patiently and repeatedly that she had watched him around the farm and that the chemistry between him and Dilly and the kittens really wasn't working. For White Chin moving away would be the best thing.

Kirstie's anguished tears still flowed and although her mother patiently explained that she would still have the kittens to love and they would fill the house and her hours, Kirstie knew in her heart of hearts that she loved their smallness, which would change as they grew up. She felt a great ache in her heart for her beloved White Chin, who had always seemed to her like no other cat she had known. She felt guilty. He had been her special companion and she had betrayed him.

## 26

## A summer of love

Gramps, who had been much excited by the prospect of having White Chin join his household, made a great fuss of him from the first moment that the tired, frightened cat emerged from his carrier.

Since the death of Granny, Gramps had taught himself to cook and now enjoyed enormously the act of preparing meals. He was delighted by the idea that now he would be able to cater for White Chin as well. The little cat enjoyed all the fuss and, once he had sampled it, the food too. White Chin didn't understand what the upheaval was about, but this bit seemed all right.

After they had settled down, and White Chin had eaten his first Gramps 'feast', the cat set off to explore the rambling old house from top to bottom and was well pleased to find an absence of animal smells. There were no bossy cats or dribbly dogs to put up with. But, look though he might, there was no trace of Kirstie either. His hopes were sorely dashed and he sat for a while, just staring straight ahead, sadly.

A cat litter tray had been placed downstairs – he was to be kept in for forty-eight hours to get used to his new surroundings – and soon White Chin made use of it, thereby claiming his territorial rights to the house. The first night, after Joan and Gramps had disappeared to their own rooms to sleep, White Chin was a little confused. He was unsure what he was expected to do. In the end he slept downstairs on a sofa in the sitting room.

The following morning Joan prepared to leave, telling Gramps that she would phone and visit shortly to make sure that all was well and for him to promise to ring her if anything went wrong with White Chin. She stroked the cat gently and looked deep into his eyes.

'Be a good boy, White Chin. I'm really sorry that we all seem to have let you down. I'm sure you'll be happier with Gramps and this will all turn out to be for the best.' With that she picked up her car keys and walked outside with Gramps. White Chin watched her go. He blinked, licking his nose, and turned away. He felt terribly unwanted.

Gramps re-entered the house and started to potter about, ignoring the cat. Gradually White Chin began to follow him around. The old man moved slowly and that suited White Chin. He felt oddly comfortable in this house and he walked from room to room in an unhurried way, thoroughly investigating his new surroundings. It felt strangely calm and peaceful. He sensed the old man was aware of him, although Gramps never stared at White Chin directly, and the cat liked him for that.

All the same, Gramps was working out what made White Chin tick, just as White Chin was taking in what Gramps was up to. He began to enjoy the way the old man talked to him all the time. The first night they were properly on their own White Chin lay on the sofa while the old man pottered about, switching things off and starting to put out the lights.

Even though the cat appeared to be asleep the old man continued to talk to him. White Chin opened an eye, a tiny little bit, to watch what was going on and after the old man gently stroked his head and mumbled some goodnight words, he listened to Gramps puffing with effort as he slowly climbed his way up the stairs. Soon after Gramps had ascended the stairs, White Chin went up to have a look and found the bedroom door open a crack. Gentle snoring sounds were coming out. He quietly jumped on the bed and settled down to sleep in a bend behind the old man's legs. The two of them woke at several points through the night and each in his own way enjoyed the other's company. Gramps would grunt hello and stretch out a blotched old hand to tickle behind the cat's ears and White Chin would rasp his tongue eagerly over the caressing fingers.

On his third day with Gramps, White Chin was let out into the garden. After investigating the immediate area surrounding the house, the little cat slowly walked through the wide-open back gate and along the lane towards the neighbouring house, which was down a further track to the right. The house was some distance from Gramps', which, as it turned out, was a great relief to White Chin. He picked up the smells of all manner of animals, some of which he didn't recognise, but some of which he knew could mean trouble. He could smell goat, donkey, goose, turkey, hen and far more worrying, dog and cat. He didn't know what all these creatures were, but he knew that dogs and cats could mean trouble for sure. After looking up the lane towards the neighbouring house, he went no closer.

White Chin yawned widely and turned back to the house where Gramps lived. As he walked through the gate, swishing his tail from side to side in a determined manner, he heard an engine buzzing away in the distance. Across a huge expanse of grass the figure of Gramps could be seen, sitting astride a lawnmower, which looked and sounded to White Chin like a smaller quad bike. The old man was wearing a battered old rust-pink sailing cap and matching trousers. The mower was racing up and down in straight lines laying flat the grass and from time to time it stopped. At these moments Gramps would laboriously get off, detach the box from the back of the mower and toss the clippings into an adjacent wheelbarrow, then remount the mower and resume his cutting. White Chin sat down and watched him for some time. On one such break the man called across to the cat.

'Come on, boy. Come over here and talk to me.' White Chin trotted across to Gramps now the irritating buzzing noise of the mower had stopped. Gramps patted the empty bit of the padded seat and White Chin sprang up next to him. They both sat there and contemplated the summer day unfolding before them. The old man talked to him for a while and then he suggested a cup of tea and a biscuit. White Chin followed him into the house, and Gramps talked to him over his shoulder about the biscuits on offer. White Chin miaowed back conversationally.

The trust and affection between the man and the cat developed more strongly with every day that passed. White Chin, without fully knowing it was happening, responded to the warmth of so much love being directed towards him. He relaxed and delighted in all that happened, come what may. He had shared a deep bond with Kirstie, but her life and all the many things that distracted her meant she was only able to spend a small part of any day with him. Now in his new life he was barely ever separated from the old man. The little cat thought, sometimes, of the red-haired girl and her dark brown Fell pony, but they seemed now to belong to another world.

Life was not without its excitements, for all that things were quieter. One day after White Chin had been in residence with Gramps for a little while Enid Batty, Gramps' eccentric neighbour, arrived 'in order to meet the new cat'. She was accompanied by two yapping Cairn terrier sisters, who bounced about a lot and were called Appley Dapply and Babbity Bumble. White Chin watched Enid but kept his distance. She made admiring comments about him to Gramps, who beamed happily like a proud father as they sat in the garden. White Chin also watched the dogs, but as long as he stayed by Gramps' side everything seemed to be all right.

The dogs in fact weren't really interested in him, as they had cats at home and were used to them. The man and woman exchanged a few sentences and then, taking turns, they started to throw a small ball for the two dogs, who chased up and down noisily after it. White Chin watched, unable to understand why they would want to do that, then decided it must be a dog thing.

Suddenly disaster struck. Enid had thrown the rubber ball quite hard towards Babbity Bumble who had caught it before it had touched the ground and the force of it had made the ball stick at the very back of her throat. The little dog started to choke. Her eyes swelled out and the lids started to close and she slowly fell over onto her side.

Gramps shouted out and rushed forward. He grabbed the dog and pushed his hand down into her mouth and pulled and jerked at the ball that was preventing her from breathing. After a huge struggle he dislodged the ball like a cork out of a bottle and slowly the dog, gulping great deep breaths, started to recover. White Chin watched as the little dog, in weak gratitude, licked the old man's hand. Enid was lavish in her praise of her neighbour for his quick action in saving her dog and both of them, laughing in relief, concluded that throwing small hard rubber balls for dogs was a dangerous activity. White Chin saw that Gramps had understood the depth of trouble that the little dog was in and the cat felt proud to be in the presence of this special man.

Over time White Chin grew into the rhythm of the rituals of life lived with Gramps. He learned the time in the morning that the old man rose, like clockwork, when he had his bath, how long he took over his breakfast and what might be the first morning treat that White Chin would receive. He learned to love the days when the sun shone, and when he would spend time out in the garden with the old man. Sometimes this meant they would just sit together under the trees, and sometimes it meant that White Chin would watch the mower tearing up and down the lawns. When it was wet the two of them sat inside and watched the rain together, while Gramps smoked his pipe and White Chin purred.

Kirstie and Buster had returned home safely and Kirstie had begged her mother to let her see Gramps and White Chin as soon as she was back, but Joan had been adamant that she would go herself and check that all was well with her father on her own. Kirstie's new term was about to start and she had things she needed to get ready for school. Upset, Kirstie begged her mother to promise that she would give her every detail of how it was with White Chin.

On her return, Joan was able to assure Kirstie that White Chin was looking better than she had ever seen him. He was sleek and happy and clearly loved the old man; and as for Gramps, White Chin could do no wrong. Joan grinned as she told Kirstie that Gramps just couldn't stop talking about 'his boy'. He seemed to have found a new lease of life.

'In fact,' Joan told Kirstie, 'Enid Batty arrived and when Gramps was out of the room she said how wonderful it is that White Chin is living with Gramps. She said something that moved me a lot. She said "I always think that until someone has an animal around them to love, part of their soul remains unawakened."' Enid had then gone on to tell Joan how with White Chin there it felt like a home again, instead of just a house.

Kirstie hugged her knees in pleasure when she heard this. All the same deep inside herself she felt a huge ache of longing for that little cat. Just thinking about him brought tears to her eyes.

Joan, anxious to stop the flow, quickly continued with tales from the Batty Ark. Enid had confessed to Joan that she was now the proud owner of no fewer than fourteen furred and feathered creatures. Their number had been increased very recently by her having won two fertile goose eggs in an auction on eBay, one of which had hatched just a month ago under her broody goose, Jemima. The new gosling had been named Cotton-tail.

'But,' Joan grinned at her daughter, 'Enid is currently calling her Princess Goose because she really does look like a princess with all her gorgeous downy feathers – well, she said, "that, or a footballer's wife!"'

## 27

# Every purpose under heaven

White Chin was sitting in the middle of the lawn washing himself, when he heard a call that was joyfully familiar to him. He jumped up and first walked, then ran towards it. His whiskers curled forward eagerly and his amber eyes opened wide from pure happiness at the sound of the beloved voice. White Chin stood briefly at Kirstie's feet looking up at her face, trembling his tail at the pure pleasure of seeing her. He thought he would burst with joy. Suddenly he felt himself being whisked through the air and found himself lying in her arms.

'White Chin, ooooh White Chin. S'wonderful to see you.' And the rest of what she said was lost as Kirstie hugged her darling cat. She held him tight and buried her head deep into his soft fur. He could feel her breathing in the smell and warmth of his body. He miaowed the strangest miaow of greeting and then his whole body thrummed with his purrs.

Was he really in Kirstie's arms? He thought she'd left him for good – that he would never see her again.

It was the first time that Kirstie had been able to persuade her mother to let her visit Gramps; at first there had been lots of new stuff at school and then Kirstie couldn't get her Mum to leave the farm, until today. Kirstie loved it that White Chin still seemed as fond of her as ever, but she couldn't fail to be aware of his special relationship now with dear old Gramps.

There was a twitchy half hour when White Chin got really muddled up during their evening meal, being unable to make up his mind whose knee he should sit on. First he sat on one and then up, and down onto the other until he saw them laughing at him, then he went and sat by himself for a while. After the family moved away from the table to sit in more comfortable chairs White Chin placed himself, rather primly, next to Kirstie on the arm of her sofa, wrapping his tail neatly around his front feet.

After a little while, he jumped down and moved across to the arm of the button-back leather chair that was always Gramps' favourite throne. At each resting place, following an initial biff with his head to say hello, a brief touch of noses in greeting or a possessive pat on the arm or the cheek with his paw, he would rumble out a deep happy purr.

While all this was going on Kirstie, Joan and Gramps talked non-stop, and Kirstie made them ache with laughter as she recounted the various adventures she and Olivia had been involved in during the summer with their two ponies.

As White Chin moved between the old man and his granddaughter distributing his favours in equal measure, Joan smiled.

'Well, White Chin. You didn't need to make it quite so obvious that I don't feature anywhere in your affections!' she observed.

'Oh Mum, you know he likes you, but he obviously adores Gramps, and I guess he loves me too. He knows that Dilly's your favourite, that's the trouble.'

'She's not my "favourite", she's just very needy. She's what I call a one-person cat. She had a bad beginning, like White Chin, and she can't help being awkward. It's her nature!' Joan pulled a wry face and laughed. Kirstie still reckoned that Dilly was her Mum's favourite, all the same.

Gramps, who'd been quietly sucking on his pipe while he listened to Joan's statement, pulled it out of his mouth.

'Well, I'm sorry but she always seemed to me a bit of a madam, that one, whereas this little fellow here,' he waved the stem of his pipe at White Chin, 'is a real gent. And he talks to me you know. But Kirstie-girl, tell

232

me how those mad kittens-in-wonderland are getting on? They'll be growing up now, won't they?'

'They're fine, Gramps, but you're right. They're growing up so fast, I can't believe how quickly they've stopped being babies. I love watching them together though, they're good company for each other. But it's funny, you know, having two's really different from just one. They don't seem to need people as much.'

The old man grunted. As the evening wore on White Chin finally curled up on the sofa, opening one eye from time to time to check that Gramps and Kirstie were still where they should be.

That night White Chin slept with Gramps, as he had done every night since they had been living alone together. Through the night and in the morning Kirstie felt a pain in her heart – something like jealousy that her beloved White Chin had not sought her out and that he had in fact chosen to sleep with Gramps. She had carefully left her bedroom door open and had been sure that at some point in the night he would come in to see her. She had kept waking up but everything was quiet and there was no sound of the light footsteps and tiny miaow she was longing to hear. As she tossed and turned thinking about it she suddenly realised that Gramps gave to White Chin everything that he most needed. He gave him his full time and his attention as well as his love, and he gave it to him properly, not just when it suited him, or he was in the right mood.

As Kirstie and Joan prepared to leave, Kirstie found

herself mumbling to her mother that she felt as if she had lost White Chin all over again, and it was now worse somehow. Her mother squeezed her hand kind-heartedly. Kirstie gave a big huggy goodbye to her Gramps and then just as they were about to get into the car she grabbed White Chin up in her arms and smothered her face in his head. She sniffed him deeply and with tears in her eyes she said in a brave voice:

'Oh White Chin, I so want you to be happy. And I do believe you are now! You are more special than I can ever tell you. You take care of Gramps won't you now? And be a really good boy!'

Late summer moved towards autumn, with its usual mixture of sunshine and rain. White Chin learned to recognise the rituals that led up to the mowing of the lawn and how much it mattered to Gramps. He also got to know the morose look on Gramps' face as he stared out bleakly at the spattering raindrops, willing the sun to shine again. On those days Gramps would sit in his chair by the window and smoke his pipe. Sometimes he would shake himself out of his gloom and talk instead to White Chin about the days of his youth, when the sun always shone and when all things were possible. They were days when music poured out of the CD player from dawn to dusk and in between the talking, Gramps would read books and snooze. On days like these, White Chin would curl up on a cushion across the old man's bony knees and curl his tail over his nose and sleep, sometimes feeling the drowsy weight of Gramps' hand on him as he too dozed. White Chin was never happier than when it rained.

But after breakfast when Gramps donned his old 'mowing uniform' it was a sure sign that the day would be long and sunny and White Chin knew they would spend it in the great outdoors. Out of the cupboard would come the rusty hat and trousers, and the worn dark-blue canvas shoes with a hole where the old man's toenail had rubbed. As soon as breakfast was finished the little cat would saunter forward with Gramps to inspect the mower and the putting out of the chair beneath the cherry tree. Once that was done, the cat would find his position to oversee the proceedings and make sure it was done well.

The two companions shared everything. They shared their meals, so although White Chin had his own food, he often had special pieces of Gramps' food too. They shared conversation; Gramps talked more than White Chin, but White Chin was a good listener. They washed together. Well that is White Chin watched Gramps go into the shower and sometimes while he showered, White Chin would lick himself too. They slept together, always, all night long, not counting the times when White Chin went on a short hunting expedition just to keep his nose in, but he always returned to Gramps afterwards through a thoughtfully opened bathroom window. And often they shared little adventures too, which each would think about in his own way.

One sunny morning Gramps had been on his mower for a couple of hours. White Chin was lying nearby in the grass by the small canvas chair, switching his attention between some birds and the old man. The only thing about the cat that moved was his tail, which twitched slightly from time to time. Gramps was sweating. As the mower neared the shade of the tree he brought it to a halt, clambered off it and flopped down into the chair, under the shade of the cherry tree. He bent down to stroke the cat and courteously enquired after his well-being. White Chin rolled over onto his back enjoying the attention and purred. Gramps took a swig of tea out of a flask he had by the chair and looked out across the lawn at his handiwork and the birdbath.

'Hey, White Chin. Look over there, but don't move, there's a good fellow!' White Chin, who was now the right way up again, was indeed watching. What they could both see was an adult bluetit facing a half-grown one. The smaller one was making a lot of noise but not doing much. It was on the edge of the birdbath, not touching the water. As the man and the cat watched – Gramps with a restraining hand on White Chin – the adult bird gently pushed the smaller one into the water. The fledgling immediately fluttered its wings wildly in the water and fluffed out all its feathers. While it was busy splashing it made a frightful squawking racket, but with what seemed like total relish. Shortly after that the tits flew off.

'Well how about that, White Chin? Now that's a first. I never knew that birds taught their young how to bath. You live and learn! Wasn't that interesting?' White Chin looked across at the old man fondly. He half closed his eyes in thought. His mind was full of the image of the birds he had been watching. And he *did* find them interesting, definitely.

White Chin spent an enormous amount of time with the old man – he had never felt this level of serenity in human company in his life before. Sometimes, on the few occasions when he did leave the old man's side, he liked to bring back a present for Gramps. In the main his presents were wood mice, shrews and voles, and on one occasion he brought back a mole. Gramps always thanked him politely for the presents, but he made it clear he liked them not to be moving, so White Chin learned that they needed to be killed first.

Enid Batty's house was a sufficient distance away from Gramps' house to be acceptable to White Chin. Sometimes you could hear her two donkeys, Miss Moppet and Mrs Tiggy-Winkle braying in the distance, a sound which Gramps said was 'quite loud enough thank you'. And if the wind was blowing the wrong way you might hear Jemima the goose on guard duty, honking her warnings, now accompanied by Cotton-tail, but otherwise Enid's ark remained secure within her boundaries and far enough away to be no threat. White Chin never visited that house as he knew from scenting the rough track down to it that there were cats there and he wanted no trouble. And the other thing was that although the two dogs never bothered with him when she came to visit Gramps, White Chin wasn't sure how they would be if he visited them.

One day Enid arrived with the dogs as usual but on this day White Chin could sense that she was upset. She walked into the house without ringing the bell and Gramps meeting her in the hallway, said:

'Enid, hey! What on earth's happened?'

'Oh, doctor! Squintina, my nineteen-year-old tabby, was stone dead when I came down this morning. Heart I should think.' And she gave a big hiccupping gulp. Gramps gave her his hankie. 'Trouble is Tabs – that's Tabitha Twitchit, her sister – isn't much younger. She was with the body all night and since I buried her sister she's been miaowing her head off. It sounds like she's calling out for her.' Enid Batty smiled tearily and mopped her eyes with the old man's hankie. Gramps waved her into the kitchen and put the kettle on. He turned to her as it was coming to the boil.

'Now then Enid, don't you fret this way. You know they always say there's a time for living and a time for dying. Nineteen is a wonderful age for a cat to reach and dying in your sleep in your own bed, what more could anyone, including a cat, hope for? One minute you're there and the next you're gone. That's a tremendous way to go!' Touching her arm, he smiled warmly at her.

'I know, it's daft isn't it?' she said blowing her nose and grinning through her tears. 'It's what I would have wanted for Squints, she was a dear soul and I'm so glad it was peaceful, but it hurts losing her. And poor Tabs is in a bad way.'

'She'll be all right, you'll see.' Gramps put his arm round her and gave her a hug, and after she had drunk her tea she left. Gramps and White Chin watched Enid walk slowly through the gate down the track towards her own place, with Appley Dapply and Babbity Bumble chasing each other noisily, in and out of the fence posts either side of the track. White Chin didn't understand what had happened, but he knew that Enid had arrived upset and that she had left a bit less so thanks to Gramps.

The year was noticeably changing. The lingering light evenings of summer faded and the short days of autumn set in, cold and rainy, and leaves blew everywhere. Gramps got tired and cross as the days got shorter and the rain depressed him hugely. He told White Chin again and again that he felt like a house prisoner and it was getting on his nerves. The continual rain had kept

White Chin inside the house for days on end too and he was now getting almost as bored with it as was the old man. Each day as he woke up he hoped today the sun might shine, but it didn't.

One day Gramps had had enough. Water had been pouring down the outside of the windows in a gushing stream caused by some blockage in the guttering and it was driving him mad. At breakfast he'd had a long grumble to White Chin.

'It's like living in a blimming fish tank. Got to sort it out, old boy, nothing for it. It's bad enough having rain without looking out through your own home-made Niagara Falls.' So after breakfast had been tidied away, and in spite of the steady drizzle of rain, the old man got out the stepladder to clamber up to the guttering. As he climbed the ladder he let out a curse as a great blob of water off one of the overhanging trees ran down the back of his neck. Shaking himself, he stretched out unsteadily to try to remove a soggy wodge of leaves that was blocking the drain-hole.

Suddenly, as he was poking away at the hole, he cried out. One enormous shout, which changed into a sort of strangled gargling sound.

White Chin, who had been in the conservatory watching through the long window, ran to the open door alarmed at the unusual sound. The old man's hand was clutching at his chest and the ladder started to fall to one side, tipping him down on the flower bed below. He fell on his back. His mouth was open, in a silent scream, and so were his unseeing eyes. He was completely still and pale and his face was covered in sweat.

White Chin rushed forward to him and sniffed all round his head. He sniffed his ears and mouth. He crawled onto the old man's chest and started to lick his cold sweaty face. He licked and licked. If he licked hard enough he could make it all right. He would make him better. He licked as if his own life depended upon it. White Chin couldn't stop what he was doing. If he stopped licking Gramps better, Gramps wouldn't exist any more and that was unthinkable. If he kept going his licking would make the old man well again and everything would be like it was before.

While all this had been going on, the rain had continued to drizzle down and the little cat was soaked through to the skin. But he didn't care. He continued with his hopeless task. He had been out with the old man for nearly an hour when Enid Batty arrived.

When Enid saw what White Chin was doing, and found that the old man was beyond her help, that he was dead, she bent over, tears running down her cheeks and cradled the cat in her arms. He miaowed once, pitifully and she rocked him against her body. Soon he wriggled free and went to be by Gramps' head once more.

Enid Batty phoned the old man's doctor to report his death and then she phoned Old Bridge Farm and after that she found a coat which she took outside and gently laid over Gramps' body. White Chin was still frantically licking the old man's face. She picked up the little cat and gently shook him, telling him that licking the old man's face wouldn't help him any more. And then she laughed shakily saying:

'Well you may ask me why have I bothered to put a coat over him. And the answer is to show respect for the dead.' But White Chin wanted to be left by the old man's head, so he could go on licking his face.

It was how *he* did respect. He padded around the side of the house knowing that he would get moved by Enid if he didn't move himself and waited. Animals know death and the little cat had smelt the death on Gramps.

White Chin opened his mouth and wailed. A few moments later he did it again. And then again. They were cries of despair from deep within him and he barely knew that he was making them. He hurt.

Kirstie and Alex had been so shocked by the news of the death of their Gramps that they were not sure how to react. They had never known anyone close to them, someone real whom they had loved, who had just gone and died. Having begged their parents to let them come over, it had been agreed they could as long as they promised to stay out of the way. The family all clambered out of the car and the two children were told to sit and wait in the conservatory.

John Metcalfe appeared at the conservatory door holding the shivering White Chin in the crook of his arm and asked Kirstie to keep him inside away from Gramps. Kirstie held the cat in her arms close to her. He was trembling uncontrollably. She looked across at Alex for support and saw him standing with his nose pressed to the window. As she followed his gaze to see what he was staring at she suddenly recognised Gramps' feet sticking out from under the coat. Enid was out there talking to their parents but they couldn't hear what she was saying and John and Joan were out of sight.

At that moment they heard their mother shout one word really loudly. It sounded like 'Why?' and it was followed by deep uncontrollable sobs. The sobs seemed to go on for ages and then from the muffled sounds they picked up, they thought that their father must be holding her. He kept saying 'there, there, there'. The sound of her grief made them go dry-mouthed. It was the first time they had heard her cry. Even in the car as they had driven over she hadn't cried, she had just been really quiet. Kirstie put White Chin down and went across and squeezed Alex's hand. He squeezed hers back and they looked at each other in silence.

White Chin gave a pitiful miaow. Kirstie bent down and cupped his chin in her hand. The misery in his face was unbearable. She stroked him and told him they would take him home with them.

Kirstie walked up to Gramps' empty armchair. She

stopped and traced her finger over the worn-out patches on the leather arms where his fingers had lain. She could smell his pipe and see the dent in the cushion where he had sat. She kicked one of the legs because the chair was empty and then a huge wave of deep sadness swept over her. She started to cry and couldn't stop. Nothing would ever be the same again. Ever, ever, ever.

## 28

## A time to mourn

When White Chin found himself back at Old Bridge Farm, he sniffed the air in a hopeless sort of way, aching for the company of the old man he had loved so deeply. He knew Gramps was dead, but in his misery he still hoped he might come back. Sometimes the little cat seemed to see the old man's shadow lurking in corners. He could feel the essence of him and yearned for his presence.

The cat's sadness was like an illness and, other than eating and necessary trips outside, he stayed curled up in a tight ball. He spent hour after hour with his paw over his eye, keeping everyone at bay by turning his back roundly against the world.

Kirstie felt deeply for White Chin. She knew how much the little cat had given over his heart. For her, too, Gramps' death was the first time someone she had loved had simply ceased to be, and it was strangely shocking. It hurt like a wound deep inside her.

Gramps had always seemed so utterly alive to her. How could someone who was so warm and laughing and so . . . so . . . so *real*, be there one minute and then suddenly the next not be there any more? Gramps, who always had time for you, Gramps who was wise and funny and who understood things in a special way so you didn't have to explain like you did to anyone else. Gramps suddenly not being Gramps any more but just stardust didn't make any sense. She now understood why her mother, when the reality of seeing the body had first hit her, had yelled out that stark, heart-rending cry of 'why?'

Kirstie watched White Chin and her heart went out to him. Tears came into her eyes as she saw his turned back and the way he didn't want to know about anyone else. It was as if he couldn't bear it. She felt like that too! His sadness looked to her just the same as her own sadness. Because of this and because she had nearly lost him, Kirstie was very careful to spend as much time as she could making White Chin know that he was loved and cherished by her.

She had learned the hard way that the trust an animal gives you is precious. It is a gift to be handled with great care. Kirstie was sensitive to the cat's sorrow, but when he let her, she made a big fuss of him. At bedtime she carried him up into her room, every evening without fail. White Chin would then fall into a deep sleep, sometimes without moving all night. Slowly, slowly, the bond between them grew and strengthened and the trust returned.

While White Chin had been grieving in his curled-up ball, the other cats had left him alone. They had seen him as sick, and had respected that. Now, as he began to recover, he had to face their different personalities. Outside Stubs wasn't much of a problem as he kept himself to himself and anyway they had an understanding of sorts. But inside, the relationships between Dilly, Dodie and Griffin were altogether another matter.

Dodie and Griffin were almost fully grown. They had matured into two fine-looking, long-haired cats with the elegant bearing of their beautiful mother. They both sported white faces and white ears, with black eye masks and magnificent black plumed tails. They were through the worst excesses of their play-hunting and play-killing, which had so disturbed White Chin when last he lived here. It seemed they had learned some feline manners, which meant that now, when their father cuffed them, they would stand down more often than not. Griffin, however, being a boy, would sometimes challenge his father and Kirstie watched these bouts of feline aggression with increasing concern. This tension was mirrored between Dodie and Dilly, and while that sometimes took Dilly's attention away from White Chin, there was a ripple of unease through the whole house. Other than the rare moments when all four cats were solidly snoozing, there seemed always to be one cat or another hissing or scampering away from trouble! The ongoing feline friction within the farmhouse often set nerves on edge – human as much as cat!

White Chin truly felt the difference in the attention that Kirstie gave him, and he returned it by staying close to her whenever she was around the house and farm. A day never passed, however, without friction of some kind taking place amongst the four cats inside the farmhouse. Griffin kept challenging White Chin as a matter of course and the battles between Dilly and Dodie increased in both frequency and ferocity. In turn this led to Dilly becoming just plain difficult with White Chin.

White Chin found all this quite hard, but his new-found respect and love for Kirstie made him prepared to put up with the annoyance. He trusted that it would all be all right.

Kirstie realised, as she watched White Chin, that the toughest time for him in the house was the evening, when Dilly tried to block his access to the bedroom. It worried the young girl, who feared that it might make him long even more for the old days back with Gramps.

One evening, when Kirstie had gone up to her room early and had intended to come down later to collect White Chin, she was astonished to hear his quiet miaow outside her bedroom window. She looked up from her bed, where she was reading, and there he was on her windowsill, having climbed up the ivy outside. She opened the window and let him in. From that time on she kept the window open just wide enough for him to come and go that way, allowing him to avoid Dilly for much of the time. This became his secret entrance and exit and gave him the space he needed.

Life for White Chin now resumed a regular pattern. During the day, when Kirstie was at school, or at weekends when she was out riding Buster, White Chin would revisit old haunts. Every now and then he would seek out Adorabelle. Sometimes she had the time of day for him and sometimes she didn't; but when she did, he found her company most agreeable and sometimes they would go hunting together deep in the woods of Troonholme Park or up on the moorland beyond.

When the days were dry White Chin spent much time out in the paddock with his old chum Buster. The bond between the horse and the cat was as strong as ever it had been, and White Chin got great comfort from his giant friend. At this time of year, with the days at their shortest and coldest, Buster was put out in his pasture during the day and brought into the stable at night. White Chin had a little ritual where he would spring up onto the stable half door and balancing on the ledge he would softly biff the pony's long face as he stood waiting for his night-time hay. They would spend long minutes together, just gently touching each other and passing time. Only they knew what exchanges they had. Buster was the gentlest creature White Chin knew. A bit like Gramps.

## War

One Saturday in early December the Metcalfe family was chatting over the table in the main room of the farmhouse, finishing a late breakfast that had somehow become lunch, when the peace was shattered by distant shouting and then loud hammering on the door. Before anyone had a chance to open it, it was flung wide by Kay Keble who thrust herself into their midst. She seemed to be in a total flap and her normally smooth blonde hair was sticking up around her head like a mad halo.

'For heaven's sakes come and help me. They're at it again and I can't go to Doug and Bernie, they'll never forgive me. Quick, we don't have much time. Please come . . . and John, for pity's sake bring a gun.'

John looked startled and stood up. He walked over and put his hands firmly on each of Kay's shoulders, as if to hold her steady.

'Kay! Calm down now. Calm down! What's this all about?'

'Men. I saw them once before. Two men. One big and a younger one. They're in the woods now, messing with snares. They didn't see me but I watched them through field glasses. They don't know I've seen them.' While she said this she dragged her long elegant fingers through her hair making it even wilder. 'Oh, do hurry, though. I haven't been able to find Adorabelle, she went out and she's still missing.'

Kirstie, who had been watching her father trying to calm Kay down with some amusement, froze as Kay said these words. Alex, hearing the magical word 'gun', rushed in from the other room. He wasn't going to miss any of that action! Kay started to talk louder about the men. Kirstie tried to say something but no one was listening to her. John was trying to talk to Joan on the quiet, but it was difficult because Kay kept following him around, waving her arms about like a windmill. Alex, now he had discovered there was to be no shoot-out, stood behind her, imitating her agitation, which infuriated Kirstie, but all the same made her giggle disloyally.

At last John got Kay to be quiet long enough for them all to draw breath. He snatched a quiet conversation with his wife and clambered into his tattered waxed coat, its big pockets bulging with unnamed objects. He went across to the agitated sculptress and put his arm across her shoulder and started to hustle her out of the house. Alex asked if he could go with them and having been told a firm no, retired back to his video game in the other room. Kirstie and her mother watched through the window as John followed Kay's red sports car in his battered old Land Rover towards Troonholme Park.

Joan hurried across the room to the phone in the hall and Kirstie heard her speaking to Bernie. Doug, it seemed, was out on some game-keeping emergency. Her mother told Bernie about the men being seen with snares in Troonholme Park Wood again. When Joan came off the phone Kirstie said, 'Mum I need to go. I might be able to help.'

'No, Kirstie! Definitely not! It's too dangerous and anyway how could you help?'

'Well I've got this feeling I might've seen them before.'

'Oh, Kirstie – really! Don't be silly. Anyway, you're not going and that's my final word.' And with that she started to head for the quad bike to take hay bales out to the sheep, mumbling that someone around the place had to keep the farm going. Kirstie called out to her above the noise of the engine, asking her where she was heading. Knowing which field her mother was bound for meant she had a tiny breathing space allowing her to get out and do what she had to do!

If she went up on Buster it would look more normal, just a kid riding her pony. Never had Buster been tacked up so fast in all his life and within ten minutes Kirstie was trotting towards the Old Bridge and Lake House.

As horse and rider entered the yard of Lake House, Kirstie looked for her father's Land Rover but couldn't see it anywhere. Where was he, she wondered? But at that moment she caught a glimpse of Adorabelle walking across the lawn towards the house with fluid grace. Kirstie grinned to herself, thinking she might have known that Adorabelle would be fine, but seeing her, at least, was a huge relief.

Gathering her reins, she urged Buster onwards. They trotted and then cantered down the main woodland track called 'the Ride'. Suddenly she saw it. The old grey car she had seen before parked on the side of the Ride. As she drew close she slowed Buster down to a walk and tried to peer in, but the windows were steamed up and she couldn't see a thing. There was a movement over to her left, close to where the snare that caught Adorabelle had been placed, but feeling nervous, Kirstie decided to keep going straight ahead. At the end of the Ride, she turned Buster around and started to walk slowly back. He snorted and jangled his bit, feeling her tension like electricity along the reins, but Kirstie couldn't relax to save her life.

Suddenly, she saw the man with white trainers who had dumped White Chin in the woods all those months before. The same younger man was with him. The older one was holding a struggling rabbit in one hand and the snare in the other. As she watched he got a knife out and slit the rabbit's throat. Kirstie pulled Buster to a halt behind a large evergreen bush, turning her head away in disgust, but something made her look back. The men, clutching all their gear including the dripping dead rabbit, were now walking briskly in the direction of their car. They were going to get away, again! Something snapped in her. She kicked the patient Buster in the ribs and he shot forward into a canter. Kirstie swung across in front of the men, waving her riding crop, preventing them from reaching the car. She stood up in her stirrups and screamed at them.

'How could you be so evil? Do you know what you've done? Not just to that rabbit I mean, but to a cat you never even saw who nearly died losing her leg in your horrible trap? And to that black-and-white cat that you just threw away in the woods like so much rubbish.' She let out one loud sob of pent-up fury and fear and frustration.

Then throwing her head back she sucked in a deep breath and shouted loudly, 'That cat – White Chin – now lives with me, and I saw what you did to him. I couldn't believe your beastly cruelty.'

All the time she was scolding them, the two men looked up at her, gawping in surprise at the sheer force of her passion. Buster now aided her by dancing in agitation at the unexpected behaviour and the men started to back off as they tried to avoid his flying feet. The pony, having got the bit between his teeth, swung his rump round and lashed out at one of them. Kirstie stuck to his back as if she was glued on and twisted her head to shout at the men once more.

At that moment the wood burst into life from what seemed like all directions. Bernie appeared on a small quad bike, followed smartly by John and Kay in the farm Land Rover and from the other end of the Ride, Doug drove up in his Jeep. The vehicles stopped and the men were surrounded and Kirstie, who was calming her agitated mount, decided now might be the time to get going. She didn't want to get into trouble so she swung the sweating Buster round and took him at a gentle trot out of the wood and back into Kay's courtyard and then on home to the farm.

White Chin wondered what on earth all the fuss was about as he heard his giant horsey friend clattering into the yard, still snorting. He went to investigate. Buster, now untacked and tied up in his stall, was covered in white foam from the sweat that had been pouring off him and his nostrils were wide and quivering. He was breathing heavily as Kirstie vigorously rubbed him down, whistling between her teeth.

The cat could tell that both his friends were agitated and that Kirstie in particular was all fired up. He walked along the stable door and chirruped his greeting to her. She looked up at the sound and quickly fastening a stable rug around Buster, she ran across to the little cat. He rubbed his head against her, comfortingly and she threw her arms around his neck and buried her face in the top of his head. The cat could feel her warm tears trickling down through his fur.

'Oh, White Chin. Those men are just so wicked and they did such terrible things to you, and it was so scary coming face to face with them. But now – I hope – everything will be put right.' White Chin purred and raising his head to her face he gently licked away her salty tears. He loved her loving him.

After all the kerfuffle had died down Kirstie had to apologise to her mother for disobeying her, but as the end result had meant that the men had been arrested, Kirstie reckoned it was worth the telling off; and Alex's face when he discovered he had missed all the action had been a treat!

It was several days before Kirstie managed to winkle further information out of her father. When he first got back to the farmhouse he had told her that with the help of the local police the two men had been arrested, but he wouldn't say any more than that. Kirstie nagged him every day until he finally gave in and told her a bit more. Doug and Bernie Wilcock had been hard at work following up the leads they had from first the snares in Troonholme Park and then the brutal deer poaching in High Fell Wood, but their biggest problem had been getting the local police to take an interest. They eventually did, but it hadn't been easy. Doug had worked hard with the dedicated Wildlife Officer and together they had found evidence that linked the two episodes, however, after the last snare had been found, everything had gone quiet.

They knew they'd have to wait until the poachers struck again and that December was a favourite month for game poachers. They had evidence to suggest that the gang that descended on High Fell Wood was part of a big deer-poaching consortium who used special lurchers trained up as savage killer-dogs.

'Dad, you don't think those horrid men will get off, do you?'

'No, I'm sure that won't happen. The snares they were using are illegal, so Doug is sure that the courts will see justice done, don't you worry. Those two won't be showing their faces around here ever again, of that I'm certain! But the signs are that they are part of the bigger gang poaching deer for venison.'

Kirstie shuddered, as she tried to blank out the cruel images of the evil things that they had done in the woods so close to her home. John saw his daughter quake and put his hand on her shoulder, gently, to change the subject.

'I never told you properly, did I, how splendid

Kay was after you had finished your performance as a rodeo rider on Buster!'

Kirstie flashed him a guarded grin, and raised her eyebrow questioningly.

'Those two no-hopers both received the wrong end of her tongue in no uncertain terms. I think they were actually more frightened of Kay than they were of the rest of us put together, and when I finally took her away you could see the relief on their faces!' His eyes crinkled in merriment as he remembered. Kirstie grinned.

'Well that means they had two angry hell-cats at them one after the other!' Kirstie said, with a hint of pride. John laughed when she said this.

'Don't you worry, Kirstie-girl. I reckon you softened them up for her!' John walked across the room towards the window and then turning, in a more serious voice he added, 'Actually, to give Kay her due, she had the bottle to make a gracious apology to Doug and Bernie for implying that they placed the snares. So let's hope she's learned her lesson about not going to the local press before getting her facts straight! The truth matters!'

As John finished this sentence they heard a sports car rattling over the cattle grid, and saw a flash of its red roof as it drove towards the window and came to a sharp halt by the door. Kirsty laughed as her Dad murmured 'talk of the devil!' but before either of them could reach the door, it was flung open wide and a wave of expensive scent floated into the room. Kay Keble stood there, shaking her long blonde hair clear of her hat and looking, in fact, positively angelic. Calling out effusive greetings to them both, she asked if she could come in, but without waiting for a reply she clip-clopped across the stone flags in astonishingly high heels. Dangling from her hand was a large square cardboard box wrapped in shiny red ribbons. She put it down on the farmhouse table with a flourish.

'There, young woman! This is for you. But you're to open it now. I had been intending it to be for Christmas but events overtook all that!'

Kirstie giggled, slightly nervously, but walked obediently towards the box. She started to open it and found inside it another box. Inside that was yet another, and then another and then tissue paper, lots of it. She touched the edge of a small card. She looked across at Kay, who smiled back at her encouragingly. She pulled it out of the layers of tissue paper and read it:

'This gift is for Kirstie. The bravest young woman I have ever met and the best friend in all the world. With thanks and love Kay.'

Kirstie shot her head up again to look at Kay who was now looking down, almost shyly. Kirstie swallowed. She put her hand back into the tissue paper and felt a small round hard sphere the size of large conker. She gasped in surprise. She pulled it out of its tissue-paper nest. It was a shiny dark brown wooden netsuke. With her fingernails she gently prized it open. It was hinged and inside as she opened it a hidden wooden platform rose up. On it, part of the same solid piece of wood, was carved a tiny, delicate, dark brown pony, just rising from his knees, his magnificent tail curled around over his back. As she held him up to her nose to see him more clearly, her eyes gleamed with pleasure at the astonishing artistry involved in sculpting something so tiny and complete from one piece of solid hardwood.

'Kay!' she whispered in wonderment, 'thank you! It's the most brilliant carving I have ever seen. It's perfect!'

# And peace, at last

Shortly before Christmas, Enid Batty was due to visit Old Bridge Farm. Kirstie badly wanted her to meet the teenage kittens and was wildly distracted just before she was due to arrive, as, typically, there was no sign of Dodie or Griffin anywhere. As Enid's noisy motor-bike and sidecar rattled into the farmyard, Kirstie discovered the kittens hiding in a brand new place on top of the bookcase. They were duly introduced and Enid was charmed, making a big fuss of them. They returned her favours eagerly, with many 'purps' and chirrups.

Part of the purpose of Enid's visit was that she had wanted the family to see photographs of Gramps with some of her many animals and this seemed the right time to come. She spread the album open on the table and they eagerly gathered round.

On the first page of the album there was a picture of Gramps, sitting in a very large armchair with the elderly cat Squintina on his knee, and Tabitha on the back of the chair behind his head, staring down at him haughtily. As they flicked on through the album they saw the old man in a series of unlikely poses with the donkeys Tiggy-Winkle and Moppet (Mrs and Miss, respectively). On subsequent pages he was seen with the well-named goat, Cross-patch, and there was even one of him apparently taking avoiding action from the rather scary looking Hunca Munca, Enid's solitary turkey.

In some of them Gramps was laughing uproariously; in some of them he was looking grumpy and in the one with Hunca Munca he actually looked quite concerned. But in all of them he looked so *very* alive. There was one where he was staring straight into the camera and pure joy was shining out from his face, which made Joan catch her breath. She couldn't stop the tears welling over. Kirstie, who had been giggling over the pictures with Alex, became aware that her mother was upset. She went across and hugged her. Enid glanced up and saw Joan look down at her daughter, wiping her eyes and laughing.

'Sorry, sorry. Silly me! What's so awful is how much it hurts now he's gone. I know he was a good age but it seems to hurt more every day, not less. I just miss him so much.'

Enid put her hand on Joan's arm in a kindly way.

'You know, Joan, Dr Parfitt was very certain that there was a time for living and a time for dying and he always said to me that dying in your own bed, or in your sleep would be a wonderful way to go.' She paused, having said that and then added swiftly, 'I know he didn't die in his bed but it *was* almost like that. It was really quick.'

'Yes and for that I'm grateful. He would have hated to leave that house. And it's true he wanted to die quickly. As a doctor he knew too much . . .' Joan's voice tailed off and she looked sad again.

'He thought death would be a terribly big adventure, you know and he also said it's always worst for the people left behind,' Enid said.

'Oh Enid, so you're saying he was always right?' Joan laughed, sniffing.

'Well, no in fact. At least, no . . . not entirely,' Enid mumbled.

Joan laughed but then she asked, kindly, 'What does "not entirely" mean?'

'Oh well, sorry, but it's just that my poor little Tabitha's died. She got some kind of cancer but it went so fast. My vet says it could have been triggered by her broken heart after Squints died. Squintina was her sister, you know. But Dr Parfitt – Gramps as you call him – assured me that Tabitha would be OK and yet, sadly, he was quite wrong about her. So now here I am, altogether cat-less.'

There were cries of sympathy all round. Kirstie then piped up with an invitation to Enid to give a home to a 'BCWA'. When Enid expressed great puzzlement as to what a BCWA might be, when it was at home, Kirstie delightedly squealed out 'A Black Cat With Attitude of course!' pointing at Dilly, who had just walked into the room with a loud, rather coarse 'mneeeeoowwww!' on her lips. She now headed towards a peacefully sleeping Dodie with the clear intention of, at the very least, disturbing the peace, if not committing murder!

Joan, as the one who was most fond of Dilly, looked a bit shocked at the suggestion, but Enid held up her hand in protest.

'No, no, no,' she said very quickly. 'And anyway in my life cats have always chosen me somehow, rather than me choosing them.'

Kirstie knew she'd put her foot in it by even half-joking that Dilly should go, so she stared at the floor with embarrassment and went a bit hot thinking about what she'd just said. Her poor mum! As she thought about it, she had one of those strange moments when everything suddenly becomes clear. She at last understood that Dilly, to her mother, was what White Chin was to her – very specially and in the deepest possible way. She could see that no matter what would happen in her future life she and White Chin belonged to each other and that nothing and no one would ever again get in the way of that. She just wished she had realised all this sooner.

Later that afternoon, as Joan and Kirstie went to the door to help Enid collect together all her bits and pieces, they laughed as they discovered that both Dodie and Griffin had climbed into her basket. There they sat, wrapped around each other, beaming up at their human audience. Climbing into baskets was something they had often done as small kittens, but it was curious to see them all scrunched up in the basket as nearly grown cats.

Kirstie drew in her breath sharply. She realised as she looked down at the kittens that something really important was happening, right now, in front of her. The kittens had somehow suddenly made everything come right. They had made their own decision! She jumped up and down excitedly and almost shouted.

'There! Look, Enid! They *have* chosen you!'

Enid grinned, but bending down she turfed the kittens out of her basket, replacing them instead with her photograph albums.

'No! No!' Kirstie protested. 'You don't understand. Don't you see, that really is the perfect solution to it all! I know I'm right, it would be brilliant for them and brilliant for you!'

With that the assembled company retired back inside the farmhouse and sat around the table to discuss whether Enid taking the kittens would really work out and be a good idea. With a bit of humming and hah-ing, Enid was at last persuaded that for her to take the kittens now would be a wonderful way of everyone ending up in a home where they would love and be loved and where they would be happy and at peace. Enid did point out that it would break her gender rule by forcing her to home a male animal, but somehow she didn't seem terribly to mind. She had fallen in love and was going home with the best Christmas present in the world!

When Enid left, not of course having a cat carrier with her, she had to put the two cats in her 'Mrs Fisher' sidecar, but as it was enclosed they were perfectly safe, and they sat together on the seat staring straight ahead curiously through the windscreen. Enid flung her leg across Jeremy Fisher's back and kick-started him into action. She turned to the assembled company and grinning broadly, waved her gauntleted hand, adjusted her goggles, tapped her black open-faced helmet for luck and roared off.

As Kirstie stood next to her mother waving Enid and her precious load on their way, Joan put an arm around her and squeezed.

'That was well done, Kirstie. I know exactly how hard it was for you to do that!'

Kirstie grinned back at her mother gratefully. It was true. It was one of the bravest things she had ever done. She loved the growing kittens and would always have a special place in her heart for them, but she belonged to White Chin.

They received regular updates from Enid on how the kittens were faring. She found the talkative, responsive, inquisitive brother and sister filled in no small part the gap left by her dear Squintina and Tabitha. She called Griffin 'Duke' because she had named Dodie 'Duchess,' which name Beatrix Potter had given to a dog, but she had never before minded using the wrong name for the right animal, and she wasn't going to start now.

After the younger cats had left the farmhouse the situation between Dilly and White Chin improved. Dilly found having only the male cat around considerably less threatening than having another female in the house. From time to time Dilly would still patrol the upper landing as if it was for her private use only and when she was in this frame of mind, White Chin simply pursued his policy of shinning up or down the ivy outside Kirstie's room. Although the human members of the household missed the two younger cats, their reward was to watch the feline peace that reigned following their absence.

White Chin learned a new and lasting happiness at Old Bridge Farm, with his beloved Kirstie. But as long as he lived, the little black-and-white cat would never forget Gramps, who had made him so happy when he most needed it.

Sometimes, now, on the right sort of night, White Chin will still go out to the wet wild woods, waving his wild tail, and walking by his wild lone. But always, without fail, he will return to the little girl he loves, in the farmhouse near the river by the old bridge.

# Acknowledgements

I want to thank all of the following people, whose contributions to the creation of White Chin have been invaluable. Among them however I would like especially to thank France Bauduin whose collaboration as an illustrator was above and beyond, and Leonie Pratt whose considerable skills allowed White Chin to truly breathe. She is an editor like NoNe other, and she taught me so much.

To you all, thank you so much.

*Marilyn Edwards (May 2010)*

Brian Alderson

Nina Atkinson

France Bauduin

Michael Dugdale

Chloe Glover

Judith Longman

Graham MacLeod

Fiona Martin

Carys Middleton

Elizabeth Newton

Philip Onions

Leonie Pratt

Daniel Randell

Andrea Reece

Sheena Robertson
Robert Snuggs
Janice Swanson
Stephanie Thorndyke
Stephanie Thwaites
Year Six (2008) of St Mary's CE Primary School,
Kirkby Lonsdale together with Jonathan Whitwell and
Sarah Oldroyd
Years Five and Six of Silverhill School (2008) and
Jane Spare
The 2nd Kendal Brownies (2008) and
Sharyn Farrar
And the whole Catnip/Bounce team who are
really special

To find out more about the author and to make
contact with her, please see
**www.thecatsofmooncotttage.co.uk**
where you can find her contact details – Marilyn
would love to hear from you!

Discover more exciting Catnip books as well as learn
more about the illustrator France Bauduin at
**www.catnippublishing.co.uk**